ALIEN SEDUCTION

TAUREAN WARRIORS SERIES

MELODY BECKETT

Alien Seduction: Taurean Warriors Series by Melody Beckett

Published by Bronzewing Books

Copyright © 2022 Melody Beckett

www.melodybeckett.com

For permissions contact: hello@melodybeckett.com

Cover by Kasmit Covers

Editing by Write Now Creative

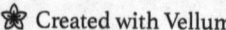 Created with Vellum

For anyone who has ever felt misunderstood.

CONTENT WARNING

This books contains:

- Explicit language
- Explicit sex scenes
- Battle scenes
- Death (on page)
- Parental death (off page)
- Large insectoid aliens

ALIEN SEDUCTION

ALIEN SEDUCTION

CHAPTER ONE

T'arq

As the engine of his stealth ship wound down, Sub-Commander T'arq Qu'Ress sighed, fatigue washing over him in waves. He was dead on his feet. Or on his ass, considering he'd been glued in this tiny cockpit for the past twelve hours. He rolled his shoulders and stretched his arms overhead, his hands brushing the ceiling. Stealth ships were the smallest spacecraft in the Taurean fleet, and the most deadly, but they were not designed for pilots who were over seven feet tall like T'arq was. After twelve hours straight of flying he was ready to relax. At the thought, a small smile lit up his face, removing the lines of exhaustion from his bronzed skin.

The thought spurring his tired limbs into movement; he did a quick check of the various controls laid out in front of him, his hands moving fluidly as he ran the final post-flight diagnostics. T'arq had changed his stealth ship to seat one, with the controls clustered to one side of the cockpit. Usually a ship of this size would have a flight engineer and a pilot, but because of T'arq's missions, when he was in the stealth ship, he worked alone.

If he was asked, he would say he enjoyed working alone, but lately he wasn't so sure. He shook his head and hit the release for the cockpit's overhead hatch, one of two exits for the small ship. The other was in the tiny cargo bay in the rear of the craft. With a hiss, the hatch to the cockpit unlocked and slid backwards to reveal one of the Starship Zataras' hangars. There were many hangars, just like this one, on the giant battleship. The walls and floor were the same pale gray as the rest of the starship, small rows of lights showing paths between the various craft that filled the large space, each parked in a designated and numbered position.

Everything on a Taurean starship screamed order, from the color of the walls to the set meal times for each shift. Once settled into the routine it was easy to let the days just slide by, the monotony only broken up by the next battle.

He supposed that was why he had volunteered to be the second-in-command to Commander Zac Qu'Rell. He had seen how determined that warrior had been and knew that, no matter what happened, life around Zac would never be boring.

And so here he was, on a mission to eradicate the evil alien Xakul menace from the galaxy.

The Taureans had been fighting the expansion crazed Xakul for decades, ever since the insectoid aliens had pressed against the boundary of Taurean space by attacking the outer planets under Taurean protection. And now the Xakul were threatening Earth, the home world of humans.

The Zataras' current mission, officially, was to patrol the

outer borders of Taurean space, but unofficially the starship was a key part of a complex intelligence gathering network, of which T'arq was a member. A team of both Taurean warriors and humans working together to prevent a Xakul invasion of Earth. Unheard of even a few years ago, but now? Now everything had changed. The Xakul were becoming more assertive and were taking more risks. The enemy had nothing to lose, and a fanatic enemy was a dangerously unpredictable foe.

T'arq unclipped his harness and stood, rolling his neck to ease the tension that had built up over the past few hours. His blonde hair flopped over his brow and he pushed it back with one large hand. He heaved himself out of the hatch and stood on one of the ship's short wings, stretching his arms overhead as he looked across the hangar.

It was late in the evening, or what passed as evening when on a starship and not a planet, and the hangar was mostly empty of people. The large space held tens of stealth fighter craft like his, plus many larger shuttles and even a few smaller freighters. Right now, most were still, waiting until their next mission.

"Pleasant run, T'arq?"

T'arq looked over the edge of the wing at his friend and commander, Zac Qu'Rell. The heavily scarred face pulled into a smile, one side of his mouth twisting and his bright green eyes holding a hint of a laugh. T'arq smiled in return and dropped from the wing, turning in mid-air to catch a handhold with practiced ease, before lowering himself to the ground. For a big warrior, he had a reputation for being light on his feet.

"Zac. I didn't realize you were back from Taurus yet." He

reached out and clasped his forearm, the scarred skin under his fingers thick where the silver lines cut the deep bronze of his friend's skin. The two warriors moved closer to touch foreheads briefly in the way of close kin. Blonde head next to blonde head. From behind they might be confused for brothers, but nobody made that mistake after seeing both of their faces. T'arq's teasing smile and dancing lilac eyes were a striking contrast to Zac's usually stern expression and inhumanly green gaze.

"It would have been a good run, except for the cloak," T'arq said, releasing his friend's arm and bending to pick up the small duffel bag that he had dropped to the hangar floor.

A raised eyebrow was the only reply.

"I've stopped using it."

"Oh?" Zac turned to walk with him, the two Taureans passing under the ship's wing and toward the rear maintenance hatch. T'arq was slightly taller than Zac, but what T'arq made up for in height, Zac countered in muscle.

"It's meant to hide my ship from the Xakul, but it drops as soon as I receive a comm signal. It's completely useless." T'arq sighed and held his hand out for the tablet that Zac held. "Sorry, it was a long mission. Let me get these checks done so we can both get out of here." Zac passed T'arq the tablet, who flicked through the pages, quickly finding the checklist he was after and working his way through the list. "A pilot is only as good—"

"—as the people who work in support." A small smile lifted the corner of Zac's mouth. "So where's the package?"

T'arq's brows drew together as he entered something into a screen. "Here." He reached into a pocket on his flight suit and handed over a small black object. "An awfully long trip for something so insignificant."

A grim smile pressed Zac's lips together. "This is not insignificant. You did well."

T'arq shrugged. "It was pretty easy, though that station AI is something else."

Zac's brows drew together. "It's just an AI."

"It's not just anything. There's something strange about Irith's Moons, Zac." In practice, Irith's Moons was an exclusive resort that provided whatever their patrons wanted... for a price. A honeymoon destination for the newly married elite? Easy. A few days of non-stop boozing and gambling? Not a problem. A bed partner or two... or more? Certainly. None of this was news to Zac, nor to anyone who had traveled through Taurean space. Irith's Moons' owners had made sure of that with a carefully crafted rumor mill.

Whoever was running Irith's Moons went to great pains to foster such a reputation. A stay on the station was highly desirable but it was nearly impossible to gain access. Although T'arq had managed it.

Zac nodded thoughtfully, standing to one side as T'arq quickly finished the checks with an efficiency that told of years of practice. "Done." T'arq turned to Zac with a grin.

"Want to go grab a drink?" Zac clapped him on the back, wrapping an arm around his shoulder and leading him away from the ship.

"I thought you'd never ask," T'arq said, thankful for any excuse to not go back to his lonely quarters. With one last look at the stealth ship, he let Zac lead him from the hangar.

———

Despite the late hour, the Zataras' all ranks bar was doing a good trade. T'arq swiped his wrist against the panel next to the nondescript door. The only indicator that this room was different to any other on this lower level was the faded sign in black lettering that read 'Bar'. The room was deep in the ship's belly, unlike the officer's bar that was many levels higher up. That place had walls made of view screens, the large multi-function screens presenting any scene the patrons desired: a tropical paradise, a regal palace, or, more often, just the view outside the starship.

Despite being an officer, T'arq had been to the officer's bar only once and had decided quickly he preferred the all ranks bar with its lack of pretense. Here the walls were the same nondescript gray of the ship, tables bolted to the floor and built to withstand years of service, and the food was hearty and the drinks strong. But, most importantly, it didn't seem to matter who you were or where you were from. Everyone belonged here.

The Taureans were used to long missions that could run to months, so they needed to decompress. Yes, there were gyms and simulation suites on the Zataras, and T'arq made good use of those facilities, but a taste of home went a long way to keeping up morale. And this small bar, deep in the belly of the giant starship, was the one place that T'arq truly felt at home.

He paused in the entry as the door slid open, the sounds of people talking and laughing spilling into the corridor. "Come on, Zac." He clapped the other warrior on the shoulder and smiled. "Let's get a drink."

Zac nodded and moved into the room, heading toward

the bar. T'arq followed, but paused as a cheer rose from one corner of the room. There were no walls of viewscreens here, just a few small screens mounted to one wall showing various sporting events from Taurus and, now that there were humans on the ship, Earth. T'arq watched as a human man jumped to his feet and started shouting at a screen. They seemed very excited about what was happening. T'arq squinted at the screen, letting Zac move ahead to the bar as he tried to see what the fuss was about.

It looked like the players were slamming into each other for no reason. No, wait. There was a ball. One player passed the ball to another who threw it the length of the field to a third player who caught the ball and turned and ran away with it. It must have been the right thing to do, because the rest of the group of humans jumped from their seats and began screaming and yelling excitedly.

T'arq snorted and continued toward his usual spot at the bar where Zac was waiting. The bar was on the opposite side of the room to the entry, meaning T'arq had to make his way through the throng of people sitting in small groups at circular tables. It was busy tonight, but T'arq still took the time to greet those he knew with a pat on the shoulder, a hug, or a wink for the more flirtatious. By the time he reached the long bar, his face hurt from the smile that had felt more forced than natural.

The bartender was busy rushing backwards and forward, delivering drinks to the waiting patrons, when T'arq arrived and slid into the seat next to Zac, who already had a drink in hand. The harried-looking bartender moved with an enviable efficiency between his patrons. His hair, shaved at the sides and left long on top, was long enough to fall to his waist in a braid, the ends dyed a deep purple. T'arq lifted a hand and received a nod in reply.

"You be wanting Karthian ale?" The bartender's accent placed him as from one of the outer planets, like T'arq. An accent that T'arq had taken great pains to lose.

Being an outsider at the Taurean military academy had been one thing, being an outsider with an accent that was associated with uncultured, uneducated farmers was entirely another. He knew it wasn't right to judge someone based on how they sounded, but he'd desperately wanted to fit in as a child a long way from home, so he'd mimicked the accent of the boys from Taurus itself.

"Thanks, Jepp. And whatever you have going for food tonight, if there's any left?" T'arq smiled apologetically, knowing the hour was past when meals stopped being served.

The bartender placed a drink in front of a customer, who waved their wrist over the scanner pad he offered. At the acknowledging beep, he returned his attention to T'arq. "I think there'll be some of that pizza the humans like?"

T'arq's stomach rumbled, and he met Jepp's amused smile with one of his own. "I think anything would do right now. Thank you."

He turned to Zac, sitting sideways on the stool to face his friend. "So, when did you get back from Taurus?"

Zac took a sip of his drink and, leaning his arms on the bar in front of him, sighed. "A few hours ago."

"How is the Supreme Commander? Does he have another mission for us?" T'arq watched the other warrior intently. Maybe this time there would be another team mission to undertake, something other than boring solo flights to deliver messages and pick up packages.

Zac shot a sharp look at T'arq, jerking his head toward the crowded room. "Not here. Tomorrow."

T'arq grimaced, realizing his mistake. He must be more tired than he thought. It was a rookie mistake to discuss secret missions in public. T'arq was a member of an elite, secret group of both Taureans and humans who completed missions that were a little... off the grid.

The bartender returned with a glass filled with foaming amber liquid, condensation running down the sides. T'arq nodded his thanks to the bartender and took a long pull from his drink.

"That's what I needed." T'arq sighed, rolling his neck from side to side.

"Squashed in that little ship again?" Zac chuckled.

"Yeah, twelve hours in one spot is enough to make my ass go numb," T'arq grumbled. He leaned forward and propped his head on his hand, stifling a yawn as he rested his elbow on the bar and waited for his food. His thoughts drifted back to the mission he had just completed. Ostensibly, he had been on a standard patrol. And, as a stealth ship qualified pilot assigned to the Zataras, that was what he would do. But his true role was a little more complex than that.

"Word has got around that you were visiting Irith's Moons." Zac put his glass down and turned to look at T'arq, one brow raised in question.

"I had engine trouble. Irith's Moons was the closest place to land while I was on patrol. That's it."

Zac's lips quirked. "If you say so."

T'arq shook his head in mock exasperation. Zac knew full

well what T'arq was doing on Irith's Moons. This little back and forth benefited anyone who might be listening.

In the months since the team's formation, T'arq had flown into some strange places. But today really took the cake, and for once T'arq didn't have the energy. He turned back to the bar in time for a plate of pizza to be slid in front of him.

"Thanks, Jepp. This looks great."

The bartender paused for a long moment in front of T'arq. "If you want some company..." Jepp let the words trail off as his gaze slid over the big Taurean. A few months ago, T'arq wouldn't have hesitated. Harmless fun with a consenting adult was just the thing to relieve some stress. But recently things had changed. No longer did he want to spend a few hot hours in the company of a man or woman or, as he had on a few memorable occasions, both a man *and* a woman. He'd wonder what was wrong with him, but he suspected he knew exactly what the problem was. Or *who* the problem was.

It was just his luck that the one person who captured his attention right now was the one person he could never have. His best friend's sister, for all intents and purposes. A recipe for disaster, unless T'arq wanted a mate. And T'arq didn't do relationships that lasted longer than one night. So that was that.

"Not tonight, Jepp." He smiled in what he hoped was a placating way and slid the pizza toward him.

"It be your loss," Jepp sang, but T'arq shook his head, and the bartender gave a dramatic sigh before heading down the bar.

A strangled noise came from Zac.

"What?" T'arq managed around a mouthful of pizza.

Zac's eyes swum with amusement over the rim of his drink. "Nothing."

T'arq swallowed. "No, really. What?" For once, he wasn't laughing.

Zac sighed. "It's like you can't help it. They just fall at your feet, don't they?"

T'arq refused to answer, shifting slightly on the bar stool. His stomach growled again and, to avoid answering, he picked up a second slice of the tasty pepperoni and cheese concoction.

"You know what people say about you?" Zac persisted. More's the pity.

T'arq swallowed and considered wiping his mouth with the back of his hand, before picking up a napkin from a stack on the bar and using that instead. He wasn't a complete animal. "Why would I know that?" He wasn't sure he wanted to know, truth be told.

"You like to have... fun." Zac turned on the stool and leaned his back against the bar, drink in one hand, one elbow resting on the bar.

T'arq's brows drew together as he contemplated taking a third slice of pizza. "And? What's wrong with that?"

Zac's expression lost all humor. "When you have as much... fun... as you do... well, you get a certain reputation."

"Huh?" T'arq looked up from his plate. A reputation? T'arq's idea of fun was to have a drink and relax with some friends. Maybe take someone back to his room. What was wrong with that? Nothing, or there hadn't been. He didn't want to admit that something might be wrong, so he just shrugged.

"Just be careful."

T'arq shot him a questioning look. "Is this about Krystal, again?"

Their eyes held for a long moment.

"You two seem pretty cozy," a feminine voice said at the same time as a hand clapped T'arq on the back. T'arq looked away, the uneasy moment not entirely forgotten.

"Hey, Laila. Welcome back." T'arq wiped his hands and slid from the barstool to wrap the human woman in a hug. She, along with Zac, was the co-leader of their covert operations team, though her official title was more of an ambassador from Earth. She and Zac were also a couple, having married in a traditional human ceremony a few months earlier.

The day that T'arq had met Laila's sister, Krystal.

"Did you come to join us?" T'arq asked as Laila stepped away.

She moved to slide an arm around Zac's waist and leaned into his side. The contrast between the two was striking; Laila's brown hair was braided tidily, and her amber eyes were warm as she looked at her mate, Zac's heavily scarred face gave him a permanent scowl, even if his bright green gaze roamed hotly over Laila as if it had been years and not minutes since he had last seen her.

"We got back a few hours ago. I'm just catching up with my sister." Laila nodded toward a table to one side of the room where a human woman with a mass of curly brown hair was sitting, engrossed in a tablet. "I'd best get back to her." She picked up a pair of tall glasses filled with a strange-looking liquid and headed back across the room.

T'arq's stomach flip-flopped. Krystal.

He had met her at Zac and Laila's wedding, and the curvy

little human had been a bundle of nerves, having only arrived in Taurean space the day before. They had danced, her much shorter frame fitting neatly in his arms, her head barely reaching the middle of his chest. But since then? He had caught only fleeting glimpses of her, usually with her head buried in a tablet, hair pushed back in a wide headband. And whenever he had seen Krystal, she had been with Zac and Laila.

He might feel lonely in his quarters, but it was worse to sit here looking at a woman that could never be his. Zac had made it abundantly clear that he was to stay away from Krystal, which normally would have made T'arq laugh. She was an adult woman who could make her own mind up, surely. But in this case, he agreed with Zac. He would stay away, not because his friend asked him to, but because he suspected she would demand more than he could give. And she was far too good for a mixed heritage, outer planets time waster like him. Best if he just stayed away.

His appetite suddenly gone, he pushed away from the bar and, bidding Zac goodbye, headed for his room.

CHAPTER TWO

Krystal

The noises in the all rank's bar were a distant hum to Krystal as she tapped away on her tablet, a line of concentration between her delicately arched brows. The clatter of a glass being put down on the table in front of her made Krystal look up sharply and drop the tablet in her hands. "Laila! You scared me."

"We're in a bar, Krystal. Put down the tablet and stop working, for once. OK?" The smile on her sister's face was at odds with the seemingly harsh words.

The all ranks bar was not Krystal's favorite place, it being loud with so many people talking and music playing. Tonight was no exception. There was a group watching, of all things, football, and at the table next to them someone had pulled out something that looked like a chess set but had three tiers. The game appearing to involve lots of standing and shouting at your opponent.

She was glad Laila had wrangled them a table, otherwise

they might have had to stand at the bar. As it was, her feet didn't reach the floor on this giant chair. That was the problem with being barely over five feet tall on a ship that was made by giants; everything was huge.

Krystal pushed back a stray lock of curly brown hair that had slipped past her headband and rolled her eyes at Laila, but she picked up the tablet and, turning, put it in the shoulder bag that was hanging on the back of her chair. "All right, though I was just thinking of a tweak to the cloak that's been giving the pilots so much grief..." she trailed off as she paused, brown eyes unfocused as she chewed on her full lower lip. There had been an issue with how light was being refracted. The Taureans had approached the problem in a way that Krystal had seen as interesting, but not optimal. So she'd made some changes of her own and was almost ready to test the prototype.

Laila snapped her fingers in front of Krystal's face. "Earth to Krystal!"

Krystal blinked, focusing on her sister. "Huh. That doesn't really have the same ring to it anymore, does it?"

"I suppose not. Here," her sister pushed a foaming neon green drink toward her across the small table. "Drink up."

Krystal picked up the glass and sniffed the liquid, her nose wrinkling at the smell that reminded her of rotten eggs. "It stinks! And it looks like—"

"Engine coolant. I know. Give it a go, OK?" Laila laughed at Krystal's wary expression and held her glass up. "Bottoms up!"

Screwing up her face, Krystal held her own glass up and took a deep breath. Since leaving Earth, Krystal had been pushed so far out of her comfort zone that she often felt adrift. Taking a small sip of the drink, she exclaimed in surprise at the taste. "Oh! It's actually not too bad!"

"Yeah, sipping is the way," Laila muttered under her breath.

"Hmm?"

"Never mind. So, how are you settling in? I know I haven't been around much this past month. It's been pretty busy for Zac and me with... stuff." Laila waved her hand around absently.

Krystal knew there was a lot about Laila's job that she couldn't—or wouldn't—talk about, and long experience showed that pushing Laila would get her exactly nothing in return, so she let it go.

"This is going to sound stupid," Krystal began, looking down at her hands as she absently picked at a torn edge of one fingernail.

"Nothing you say would ever sound stupid, Krystal." Laila tilted her head. "Is everything ok?"

No, it hadn't been ok for a long time.

Krystal hadn't wanted to worry Laila, not with everything she had gone through recently. Surviving the attack on Mars by the Xakul, being sent to the other side of the galaxy to join forces with the Taureans... Krystal's problems had felt insignificant in comparison. And then when Laila had met Zac and had finally found a small piece of happiness, well, Krystal wasn't about to unburden herself and spoil that for her only family member.

But now? Here she was, on a spaceship for crying out loud, and she still felt unsettled. It didn't seem to matter where she was. There was something missing.

"I thought it would be different," she blurted, avoiding Laila's gaze.

"Different? What would be different?"

"I thought that once I was away from Earth that I'd feel more at ease, you know? I thought getting away from all the protestors and the riots would help. But I don't think being on Earth was the problem."

Laila cradled her drink between her hands where they rested on the table. "What was the problem?"

And wasn't that the million-dollar question? Working in a factory for Space Force had been Krystal's job until a few months ago when Zac had organized for her to join the engineering team on the Zataras. And it *was* an enormous improvement from her life on Earth, which had become... difficult. Protestors were targeting people who worked for Space Force, and even civilian contractors like Krystal weren't safe. Every day, she wasn't sure if they would accost her as she tried to enter the factory. It had become so bad that a military escort had to be used, that had been after one worker was badly injured.

At best, the protestors didn't approve of what they saw as interference in Earth's affairs by an alien race, and at worst they didn't even believe that the Taureans and Xakul existed. And the second type was the most dangerous of the protestors. Some groups had even been named terrorist organizations after starting riots.

It was the Mars Incident that started the entire debacle. The Xakul had attacked the red planet, destroying almost the entire human colony. The survivors had been sent to join forces with the Taureans, which played right into the hands of the conspiracy theorists who claimed the lack of survivors on Earth was evidence the attack hadn't happened, or that nobody had died, and even that the Taureans did not exist. It didn't seem to matter what evidence was put forward by Space Force, it still wasn't believed.

But Krystal knew all too well what had happened. Laila had been one of the few survivors of the massacre and, for her troubles, Space Force had sent her to learn from the Taureans how to defeat the insectoid Xakul. Then Laila had been declared dead by Space Force while on a mission with the Taureans. Useful as a pawn and nothing else.

Any goodwill Krystal had for Earth's military had gone, and all she'd wanted to do was to join her sister. And it didn't matter if it was in space. It had taken a few months, but she had finally made it, with Zac's help.

Even so, she didn't feel totally at ease. She felt like something was missing, and seeing Zac and Laila so happy together had started a suspicion of exactly what that missing thing was.

She huffed a breath out. Whatever. At least she had the advanced Taurean technology to geek out on, right? And that's what she did. She lost herself in her work, avoiding any kind of social interaction like this.

"Krystal?" Laila's voice broke through her thoughts, and she jolted upright in her seat.

"Sorry! Did you say something?" Krystal had a habit of disappearing into her thoughts. It sometimes felt like she had blinked and an hour had passed.

Laila smiled. "I should be used to it by now, right? Always daydreaming."

"Well, you know me." Krystal shrugged, forcing a smile. It wasn't a dream, more a nightmare ever since the Xakul had appeared.

"Yes, and we've hardly seen each other in almost a year. I want to make sure you're OK." Laila leaned forward in her seat and reached to pat Krystal's hand, the motherly gesture bringing a lump to her throat, and she swallowed. As much as the big sister routine bugged her, she really had missed Laila. She took a sip of the engine coolant drink again and swallowed, the burning sensation becoming a warm glow. She dropped her gaze to look into the depths of the glass, watching as the colors swirled together like a stormy sea.

A group of Taureans nearby broke into loud laughter, one of them singing a few lines of a song that sounded suspiciously like a sea shanty. Krystal glanced at them, watching as they laughingly threw arms around each other and swayed from side to side. Their heads were close together, close-cropped hair and dark uniforms with the colored arm bands that marked them as Taurean warriors.

Krystal looked down at her own lumpy boilersuit and picked at a loose thread on the too-large cuff.

"It's all right for you," she said, tracing the rim of her glass with one finger.

"What's all right for me?" Laila hummed along with the tune the Taureans were singing, smiling absently.

"This." Krystal gestured around the room. "Look at them all." Everything was just a little off here. The furniture was too big, the clothes too big, the people. Everything.

Laila looked around and back at Krystal, a puzzled look on her face. "What about them?"

"They're huge!" Krystal choked out.

Laila laughed. "Really? That's what's bothering you?" She

took a swig of her drink and swallowed, pulling a face at the strong flavor.

Krystal scoffed. "I'm barely 5'3", Laila. You're the one who scored all the height in the family." Krystal kicked her legs under the table. "My feet don't even touch the floor!"

Laila bit her lip to stifle a laugh. "Ok, that's true. But they still tower over me."

Krystal raised an eyebrow and sat back in her seat; arms crossed over her chest. "Sure. At least you can reach all the controls without a step stool."

Laila slapped a hand over her mouth, eyes twinkling.

"Oh, laugh all you want, giraffe girl." Krystal used the childhood nickname that Laila had earned after her growth spurt at twelve. "It makes me feel so much better."

Laila bit her lip and got herself under control. "I'm sorry, Krys. It is kind of funny, though."

"Not when you have to carry around a step stool all the time, and your tools and all the other gadgetry. When you don't read Taurean and the translator doesn't work to translate written languages and—"

"All right, I get it." Laila held up a hand. "Do you want me to talk to your boss about it?"

"No!" Krystal sat bolt upright in her chair, waving her hand in a chopping motion. "No. It's bad enough that she thinks I'm a child because of my height. Can you imagine what she would think if my big sister was to talk to her?"

"Yeah, I see how that wouldn't help." Laila grimaced.

Desperate to move the conversation away from herself, Krystal swiveled in her chair, searching the room and zeroing in on the only other familiar figures in the bar. "Was that... T'arq... you were talking to at the bar?"

Laila's eyebrows shot into her hair. "Don't forget Zac, too." She smirked. "But I thought you weren't paying any attention?"

Krystal fidgeted, looking at her hands and willing her face to not go red. "I wasn't," she mumbled, flushing.

Would she ever outgrow her intense blushing? It was embarrassing.

"Sure." Laila drew out the word in a sing-song voice that said she thought the exact opposite.

Krystal looked up; lips pursed. "All right, so I looked. Is there anything wrong with that?"

Laila's smile dropped, and leaning forward, she braced her forearms on the table. "Krystal, I just don't want you to get hurt."

Krystal straightened in her seat. "What makes you think I'll get hurt?"

"Don't get testy. T'arq has a reputation, that's all."

"Oh?"

Laila shrugged. "He has a lot of... partners."

Krystal fought not to laugh at the uncharacteristically prudish statement. "You mean he likes sex?"

Laila sat up and glared at her. "Yes, that's exactly what I mean. No need to be so blunt."

Krystal couldn't help but laugh. "And why do you think I will get hurt?"

"He doesn't do relationships, Krystal."

"And I do?"

"Well, have you ever had a boyfriend? A girlfriend? Any kind of love interest?"

Krystal shook her head. "You know I haven't. Well, apart from that one guy in college who I realized was just using me, so I would do his homework for him."

"See what I mean? You are inexperienced and he is—"

"The exact opposite?"

"Yes!"

"So why wouldn't I want him to help me get experience?"

Laila's mouth dropped open, eyes wide, and the blood drained from her face.

"It was a joke!" Krystal patted her sister's hand reassuringly, the role reversal not lost on her. "It's not as if he even knows that I exist. And I'm smart enough to know to avoid the playboy type." She used her fingers to make air quotes as she said the word playboy.

Laila breathed a sigh of relief.

They sat in silence for a minute, each sipping their drinks.

"So, you were telling me about that cloak you've been working on?" Laila broached.

Krystal brightened at the change in topic, quickly catching Laila up on the work she had been doing and how she thought it might help.

When she had finished, Laila regarded her.

"Oh. What's that look for?" Krystal asked, arms crossing over her chest.

"I have an idea. Meet me in hangar bay nine before your shift tomorrow morning."

———

When Krystal arrived at hangar bay nine the next day, it was to find Laila and a small group of Taureans standing around a stealth ship. Or what Krystal assumed was a stealth ship, as she hadn't had the chance to work on one yet. The problem with being a human civilian contractor to a Taurean military starship was that they barely gave her anything interesting to work on. She was a glorified maintenance worker, fixing cleaner bots and replicator units. She wasn't allowed near anything that flew.

But she had needled and nagged until she had been allowed to work on the one thing that her boss had assumed she could not fix—the cloaking problem. In her own time, of course.

Krystal crossed the busy hangar, dodging and weaving out of the way of small automated robotic carts and groups of Taureans so tall they seemed like giants. Would she ever get used to simply how big they were?

She made her way toward the group, Laila spotting her and turning to smile. It was at this moment that Krystal's luck, or lack of, showed itself and she tripped over the too-long hem of her uniform and fell to her hands and knees. In front of the entire group of extremely competent warriors. Including T'arq.

Taking a deep breath, she sat on her heels, her face hot. Great. Her palms stung where she'd landed and she'd just made a complete idiot of herself—

Large hands scooped her up and placed her gently on her feet.

"Oh!" Krystal gasped, stumbling a little and reaching out to brace her hand on a very firm abdomen. She blinked, realizing she was staring at a very broad, very firm, chest encased in a tight, black t-shirt that left absolutely nothing to the imagination.

She looked up to see T'arq's concerned lilac eyes. Krystal

swallowed; her throat dry as she desperately tried to recall the value of pi. Nope, it was gone. She had officially been stunned stupid by a beautiful man. Alien. Whatever.

A little voice whispered in her mind, *climb him like a tree.* She flushed a deeper red, if that were possible, and desperately tried to get herself under control.

T'arq lifted a hand to push back a lock of hair that had escaped her headband, and that was it. She completely lost the ability to speak and stood still, unable to look away from his face. His rather handsome face, if she was truly honest with herself.

"Are you all right? That was quite a fall." He didn't wait to hear her answer, instead dropping to his knees in front of her and taking her hands in his much larger ones to examine them. Kneeling, he was as tall as Krystal, and didn't that just make her feel... well, she wasn't sure how that made her feel. "You've grazed your palms." He turned his head to call out, "CJ? Bring the medi-scanner!"

"Right here," a human woman slapped the small, oblong-shaped device into his outstretched hands. Her eyes raked over Krystal, a blank expression on her face as cool as the white blonde of her hair.

T'arq took it without comment and switched it on, waving it over Krystal's hands. She watched as the skin closed up, new pink tissue forming rapidly.

"Wow, that's pretty cool. How does it work? Do you know what it uses to stimulate the body? It must work on a micro-cellular level." She snapped her mouth shut. "I'm babbling."

T'arq grinned, their faces at the same height, and her breath caught. He was stunningly gorgeous. No man... alien... whatever... had any right to be that attractive. Snapping off the device, he handed it back to CJ, not looking away from Krystal.

She flushed and looked down. T'arq followed her gaze, catching sight of the legs of her boiler suit that were caught over her boots.

"I see why you fell. I'll fix it," he said, pulling a knife from a sheath on his belt—how many of those did he have on him?—and neatly sliced through the fabric to shorten the hem on first one, then the other leg.

"Um, thank you," Krystal said when he looked up at her with a grin, proffering the trimmed fabric.

"You're welcome," he said, standing to his full height.

She gazed up at him, realizing that her head barely hit him mid-chest. He stilled, the smile falling from his face as he reached a hand to smooth a fallen strand of hair back from her forehead.

"Ah, T'arq?" a deep voice asked.

"Shit!" Krystal sprung back. Everyone hadn't been watching this, had they? She looked around at the group. Oh, they had. How embarrassing.

T'arq stepped slightly in front of Krystal and addressed Zac. "We're done," he said, shooting a look at Krystal. He added quietly, "For now." And winked.

He actually winked at her!

Her eyes widened as she looked up at him, and then shot a glance at Laila, who was mouthing something at her and shaking her head slightly. Krystal walked over to join her where she was leaning against a portable ladder on wheels. "So, why did you want me to come down here?"

"Have you looked over any of the ships yet?"

Krystal shook her head. "No, they've had me do maintenance."

"But you're allowed to work on the theory for the cloak, right?"

"Yes, that's right."

"What good is that without getting to look inside an actual ship?" Laila smiled and gestured at the stealth ship with one hand, pushing off from where she was leaning against the ladder and making her way towards it. "Well? Are you coming?"

"Really?" Krystal trotted after her sister, quickly catching up and settling into walk next to her.

"Yep. I figured you probably needed permission, and T'arq's ship is right here. Why don't you have a look around?" Laila reached the stealth ship and pressed the release for the lower entry, a hatch sliding open and a ladder descending.

"He wouldn't mind?" Krystal chewed on her lip. She didn't want to cause any problems.

"Somehow I don't think so. But remember what I said." Laila dropped her voice. "Be careful around him."

"I have exceptional hearing, you know."

Oh, dear lord. Could this day get any more embarrassing?

CHAPTER THREE

T'arq

Laila had warned her about him? T'arq watched, fascinated, as Krystal's cheeks turned a bright pink. As his gaze skimmed over her face, her color deepened, spreading down her throat. He wondered just how far down it went.

"What have you done to make her angry?" Zac asked.

T'arq turned toward him, breaking his gaze from the two women, an uncomfortable feeling settling over him.

"Angry?" His gaze shot back and forth between Zac, who was scowling at him, and Krystal. Surely he had done nothing to upset her?

"Yes, why is she red?" The bright green gaze of the other man's intelligent eyes speared T'arq, and he gaped, mouth opening and closing like a fish. He hadn't upset her, had he?

"She's red because she's embarrassed," Laila hissed as she approached them. "And she's getting more embarrassed at the two of you making a fuss."

She was right. Krystal had ducked her head and disappeared around the far side of the stealth ship, out of view, but not before he'd seen her grimace at the attention. T'arq swallowed and looked at his feet. He felt like a child. He was normally so good at reading people's reactions, including the humans on his team. At knowing what people were thinking and feeling. But there was something about the small woman that had him second-guessing himself.

What had he done that Laila had felt the need to warn her sister about him?

He didn't want to think about it. He turned and walked toward the ship, needing distance and time to clear his mind.

He slid his hand over a recessed panel which glowed at his touch and, with a hiss, the hatch on the top of the stealth ship opened. T'arq reached up, hands above his head, to grab the wing, intending to pull himself up to the cockpit, but paused as the sounds of footsteps approached. He turned.

"How does it work?" Krystal's brows drew together in concentration as she stared at the panel T'arq had just touched.

He dropped his arms, turning to lean against the side of the ship. "It's activated by the heat of my hand, and by touch."

"Hmm," she murmured, running her hands over the panel.

T'arq watched as she tried to get the panel to repeat what it did for T'arq, grunting in frustration when it wouldn't work.

"Here," he said, reaching for her hand and covering it with his own. Her small palm lay flat against the ship, his larger one completely swallowing it as he gently pressed her fingers flat.

"Oh!" she gasped, stiffening and lifting her head so her wide open brown eyes met his.

His lips twitched at her reaction, certain this time that he was reading her correctly. He smiled and her eyes opened even further, a feat he thought was nearly impossible, and her mouth dropped open.

"Everything all right? I didn't mean to upset you."

Her gaze dropped to his mouth, and he couldn't resist flicking his tongue out to lick his bottom lip.

"It's OK. I should be used to it by now," she sighed.

"Used to what?" he asked, holding still as he willed himself not to move closer. Her hand was cool under his, the fingers delicate and small compared to his larger ones.

"Laila wanting to protect me. I'm sorry about what she said," Krystal's chin lifted, a note of steel entering her voice. "I can look after myself. I'm not a child."

He grinned, white teeth with just the slightest hint of fang peeking out over his bottom lip. "Oh, I am aware of that, little mouse."

"Little mouse?" she asked with raised eyebrows.

He grinned. "It suits you."

She looked down at herself. "The only thing little about me is my height."

His smile spread. "You are diminutive, yes. That's not what I meant, though."

"Oh? What did you mean?"

T'arq paused, watching as spots of color appeared on her cheeks. Definitely not angry, then. "Maybe I'll tell you sometime. Until then, you can wonder."

He pulled his hand away from where it had been covering Krystal's and felt an immediate sense of loss. Krystal seemed surprised that her hand was still touching the ship, but exclaimed in pleasure when she saw the panel had lit up. T'arq smiled indulgently, amused that Krystal had forgotten him as she examined the panel's display. He took a step back to see Zac approaching them.

"I'm needed on Taurus with," he began as he approached, pulling a tablet from his pocket and flicking through the screens, scowling.

"What? Again?" Krystal muttered over her shoulder, still looking at the display panel.

"Yes, it's our job," Zac said, offhandedly as he typed something out on the tablet.

"I thought she was an advisor." Krystal turned away from the ship and crossed her arms across her chest. "It seems like an awful lot of traveling."

Zac's hands paused in typing the message, and leveled a narrow gaze at her. When he offered no reply, she raised her eyebrows and made a face at him. Zac snorted and shook his head and turned to T'arq, dismissing Krystal, who huffed in displeasure at being ignored.

"I need you to keep an eye on Krystal."

"I'm right here, you know! And I can look after myself," Krystal protested.

"Why?" T'arq asked, nodding toward the woman in question. "She seems able to take care of herself."

"Again. I am right here!"

T'arq's lips twitched as he avoided looking at her.

"That's debatable," Zac said, lips twisting in amusement. "She will work and work and forget to eat and then fall asleep at her station in engineering."

"Argh! Once! I did that once!"

"The Xakul threat is increasing. They're becoming increasingly more unpredictable." He rubbed a hand over his face, exhaustion apparent as his smile dropped. "Look. I just have a bad feeling, and I don't want Laila to worry. You'd be doing us both a favor if you could make sure Krystal looks after herself and doesn't get into any trouble."

T'arq managed, with difficulty, to suppress a smirk as the woman in question stomped her foot. Zac's request was obviously made from a place of familial concern, but she was an adult after all, and perfectly capable of making her own decisions. But he found her frustration amusing and couldn't help teasing her.

"All right," he said, clasping Zac's arm in farewell, "I'll do my best to keep her out of harm's way."

Zac thanked him and left; his departure ignored by Krystal who turned on T'arq with fury radiating from every pore. "Oh, for fuck's sake! I'm done!"

T'arq's laughter burst from him like a dam. One second he was laughing and trying to breathe and the next he had a furious Krystal waggling a finger in his face.

"Think this is funny, do you?" Her dark brown eyes were furious, and her hair was wild around her shoulders, matching her mood. The curls looked so soft, and he wondered what they felt like. Without realizing what he was doing, he reached to touch one.

"Oof!" She smacked his hand away. "Stop treating me like a child!"

"Stop acting like one and I will." T'arq walked away, still chuckling, heading to the far side of the shuttle. Krystal followed him.

"I do not act like a child!"

"And stomping your foot in anger is an adult behavior where you are from?"

She spluttered and straightened to her full height. Which wasn't very tall, he noted. Not compared to him. He stopped walking, out of sight of the rest of the team, hidden as they were by the small ship, and turned to face her. She pulled up too late, almost running into him. She was close enough to touch, and his hands moved as if they had a will of their own.

"Lost for words?" He winked, his large hands settling on either side of her waist. He breathed hard as his fingers sunk into the soft curves of her hips, his thumbs almost touching at the front as they pressed gently into her stomach. She was deliciously curvy, all thick thighs and generous hips that were hidden by the monstrous uniform she wore.

His cock thickened uncomfortably in his tight flight suit as he contemplated what she would feel like without her clothes on. What she would look like...

She took a step toward him, her head not even reaching his shoulder, her mass of wayward curls brushing his chest. He breathed in, surrounded by an unfamiliar, but delicious, scent.

"Mmm. You smell good," he murmured softly, his pants becoming impossibly tight.

She shivered and lifted her head. "It's coconut."

"What?" His brain struggled to make sense of her words, his thumbs brushing up and down her stomach as he gently pulled her closer.

"The smell. It's my shampoo. It's coconut." She swayed toward him, head tilted back and arms braced against his torso.

"Oh, it's much more than that, little mouse," he whispered against her ear.

"Ready, T'arq?" A deep voice broke into their little bubble.

"Shit! Shit! Shit!" Krystal stiffened and tried to pull away, T'arq releasing her reluctantly.

"Nice timing, Domik." He might be the most intelligent of the team, a walking encyclopedia as CJ called him, but Domik really had awful timing.

Krystal stepped away, trying to smooth her hair and looking around with wild eyes. T'arq adjusted himself unhurriedly. Krystal's gaze fixed on the crotch of his pants and he smirked.

"Have dinner with me."

"What?" Her brows drawing together in confusion before lifting as the reality of what they had just done hit her. She crossed her arms against her chest and pursed her lips.

"Dinner. You need to eat, right?"

She shifted her weight to one side and cocked her hip. "You think that just because of that," she waved her hand around between them, "I'm going to put aside my anger?"

"Come on, Krystal. What do you have to lose? It's just dinner."

She stilled, something shifting in her expression as she shook her head. "No. It's never just anything with you, T'arq."

An uncomfortable pressure built in his chest, and he shifted to take a step away. Had he so completely misunderstood her? Had she not been a willing participant? Was he so used to getting his own way that he had pushed her into something she didn't want?

His stomach flipped at the thought. "I'm sorry. I didn't

realize you weren't interested," he said, taking a step backwards to give her more space.

Her eyes shot to his. "What?"

Laila and Zac appeared from around the side of the shuttle, having thankfully missed the interaction between him and Krystal.

"Hey, Krystal. Zac told you we're heading off again?" Laila approached, oblivious to the tension between her sister and T'arq.

"Huh? No, he's asked T'arq to babysit me," Krystal replied, crossing her arms over her chest. "Thanks a lot."

"What?" Laila turned to look at Zac, shaking her head.

"Why would you want to sit on a baby?" Zac asked.

Krystal and Laila shared a look, Laila gesturing for Krystal to join her and the two women walked away to talk quietly, heads close together.

Zac shook his head. "I will never understand humans."

T'arq watched the two women for a long moment, before turning away with a sigh. Whatever had just happened with Krystal felt unfinished. He pushed his hair back from his forehead and sighed. She might not want to have dinner with him, but he needed to clear the air at some point. He'd just have to find her later. After she'd had some time for her anger to diffuse. Hopefully.

T'arq turned to Zac. "So, what's the plan while you and Laila are away?"

He, Domik and Zac pulled up some stray chairs to sit seemingly casually. They didn't have a base of operations. They didn't even have an official name, instead just calling themselves the team. Their meetings changed location regularly, aiming to appear just a group of friends who were chatting while they worked.

Today they were next to T'arq's stealth ship in the hangar he had left only the night before. The lights were now set to the daylight setting, and workers rushed about readying craft for departure and completing routine repairs. Nearby, a maintenance team was repairing a scrape on the floor of the hangar. The dull gray of the walls and floor was replicated in the uniforms the starship's crew wore, only a colored band showing their role. The noise of their laser cutter, and that of the transports moving around the hangar, stood in stark contrast to the quiet of the night before. All the better to cover their voices.

The team often met on the shuttle that Domik and Oren flew on cargo runs, which was their cover. The brothers often took the slower cargo shuttle on supply runs to smaller stations that the Zataras couldn't dock with. But that shuttle was in for maintenance today and currently crawling with mechanics.

"That information you collected yesterday from our contact on Irith's Moons is why we're heading off so soon. We think the Taurean Purists are planning an attack. We don't know exactly where or when, but we have a lead that Laila and I will follow up."

T'arq shot a look at the two human women, before leaning in slightly and saying in a low voice, "Do you think that it's wise to take Laila? You know how they feel about humans."

Zac scoffed. "Just try to keep her away."

T'arq nodded with a small laugh. Laila was a capable fighter in her own right, and the co-commander of their secret special forces team alongside her husband Zac, who had learned his lesson early about trying to keep her away from the action.

But this mission? The Taurean Purists were fanatics, and that made T'arq nervous. The group had popped up seemingly out of nowhere after Taurus and Earth had formed an alliance. They were extremists who believed that forming alliances with "lesser races" watered down the strength of Taurus. The most extreme factions had been responsible for death threats to humans and Taureans working alongside them.

And a death threat to the Supreme Commander himself, Karik Za'Rell, if rumors were to be believed.

"What have I missed?" Oren pulled up a chair between T'arq and Domik and settled into it gracefully. The older Taurean intelligence operative moved so quietly that he made even the battle-hardened T'arq jump in his seat.

"Stop sneaking up on people!"

Oren leaned forward to clap him on the back with a chuckle. "It's part of the job, T'arq." His piercing aqua blue gaze sparkled with laughter, the lines at the corner of his eyes crinkling. The older brother of Domik, they were very different in looks. Oren shaved his head to silver stubble, which stood out in bright contrast to his skin, which was the typical Taurean bronze. Domik was much darker in coloring, his skin more dark brown than bronze. His hair was almost black, shaved at the sides and longer on top, so much so that he had pulled it back in a braid that hung to his shoulders so it wouldn't flop over his face. Where Oren's eyes were aqua blue, Domik's were almost black. It was hard to believe they were brothers, but they were.

"You haven't missed much," Zac said. "Laila and I are heading off to chase up a lead on the Taurean Purists' threat. We need you and Domik to head to Irith's Moons to see what you can find out. T'arq can't go with you. It will look too suspicious if he returns so soon."

T'arq shifted in his chair. He hated being left out of a mission, but he understood the reasoning behind it. It didn't mean he had to like it.

"What's the cover?" Domik asked.

Zac smiled. "It is a pleasure station, Domik. What do you think?"

The giant Taurean looked blankly at Zac.

"Oh, never mind. Can you two think of something?"

Oren rubbed his hand over his whiskered cheek. "Irith's Moons doesn't get supplies from the... usual sources," he mused. "They like to keep their clients' identities a closely held secret, and are suspicious of outsiders. Nobody really knows who owns the station, not really. The primary contact is an AI, and the workers never see the owner. There are more rumors about who actually runs the place than I can keep track of." Oren shrugged, looking around the small group. "It's difficult to get an invitation; it was pure luck that T'arq was allowed to dock there after having," he shot a wry look T'arq, "engine trouble."

There were a few groans.

"What about healthcare?" Domik asked.

The three others stared at him.

"Well, the people who work there need to have check-ups, don't they?" he asked.

Oren sat back in his chair, eyebrows raised, a slight frown on his face. "It's actually a pretty good idea. I don't recall the station having more than an automated medical center. The only problem is that we don't have a doctor. CJ is a good medic, but she's not a doctor. If she actually has to do medical exams, our cover will be blown immediately."

"The solution is obvious," Domik said. "Let's bring the human doctor, Amelia."

"No," Oren said, slashing the air with his hand. "It's too dangerous."

"It makes sense," Zac said, ignoring Oren's protests. "There are humans on Irith's Moons, and it would give the perfect excuse. How else would they get the actual medical care they need? Taureans aren't familiar with the differences between us and humans, and humans aren't used to trusting AIs yet."

"No." Oren's scowl was murderous.

"Can you think of a better solution?" Zac asked.

Oren clamped his lips shut, glaring at his commander.

"I didn't think so. You're the closest to Amelia, you convince her. You leave as soon as we can arrange it."

Oren stood stiffly and stomped away; his hands clenched in fists as he left the hangar.

T'arq's gaze followed him, surprised at the uncharacteristic display. "What's wrong with him?"

Domik answered, not looking up from the tablet in his hands. "Nothing. He's just in knots over his feelings for Amelia."

That was new.

Domik looked up from his tablet. "He moped for weeks after he crashed on Earth. That only stopped when she was posted to the Zataras. But something must have happened at

Zac and Laila's wedding. Ever since then, he has been very short-tempered whenever her name comes up."

T'arq's eyebrows shot into his hairline. He couldn't imagine the usually calm and reserved intelligence officer *moping* over a woman. He would never fall in love and make an idiot of himself. No way.

He laughed at the thought as he headed off to the training rooms for his daily workout.

CHAPTER FOUR

Krystal

She had made it back to engineering just in time to start her shift. That had been three hours ago and, ever since then, she'd been fiddling with a cleaner bot that just would not behave. No matter what she did, the bot would not do what she wanted. Frustrated, she growled and kicked it. It gave a small, sad bleep.

"I'm so sorry!" She immediately dropped to her knees and picked up the little bot, cradling it in her arms. "I didn't mean it, really."

"So you talk to bots, too."

She froze. The deep voice sending a shiver through Krystal. T'arq. She turned to take in the familiar, albeit sweaty, blonde head that peered at her around the corner.

Oh, dear lord. Of course he was here to witness her talking to a bot.

She had spent the last few hours trying to hold on to her anger, but reason had prevailed and she had admitted to herself, albeit reluctantly, that Laila and Zac had only been trying to help. And T'arq had been trying to do what, exactly?

She didn't think he was playing games with her, but why else would he say those things? Why would he touch her like that? Her waist had felt cold without the feel of his enormous hands holding her. So, no, she wasn't angry anymore.

Krystal's mouth dropped open as T'arq moved into the room. She took in the muscular body encased in a sweat-drenched shirt that clung to his torso. His arm muscles bunched as he lifted an arm to push back his sweaty hair. The hem of his shirt lifted to show a tantalizing glimpse of taught stomach, the edges of which formed a tight vee that disappeared into the waistband of a pair of scandalously short shorts. The fabric pulled tight across those bronzed thighs, the thighs she had dreamed about straddling. He had muscles on top of muscles. Even his calves were worth ogling.

She gave herself a mental shake and bent to put the bot down on the ground. It immediately released a series of bleeps, moving backwards and forward rapidly on its little wheels, and squirted a stream of cleaning fluid all down the front of Krystal's uniform.

She sighed.

Great, just great. Now she looked like a complete idiot in front of him. Again.

There was nothing for it but to get this over with, soaked uniform and all. "Yes, T'arq? I talk to bots. As you can see." Krystal stood and pointed at the bot that banged idly against her foot, before scooting away to get stuck in one of the room's corners. She wondered if it was trying to hide, a feeling she sympathized with.

The big Taurean's teasing grin dropped as she

straightened, his lilac eyes darkening as he took in her soaked front. Krystal looked down at herself, only just noticing how the thick fabric was clinging to her skin. She frantically plucked at it, trying to pull it away from herself. A choked groan had her quickly glance up to see T'arq's face twisted in a pained expression.

"I need to change," she muttered, still trying to pull the fabric away from her skin.

"Yes, that might be a good idea." He cleared his throat, staring at a point somewhere over her head.

"What are you doing down here? Was it because of Zac and Laila? You really don't need to check in on me." She checked her watch. Oh! It was half an hour after the time she usually ate. The mess would be closed by now. She grimaced. "I thought we agreed I could look after myself."

He grunted, still focused on her chest. "Yes, of course."

"Good, so you won't tell Zac and Laila that I missed lunch?" she added under her breath. "Again."

"Huh?" He looked up from her chest with difficulty. "No? Why would I do that?"

She breathed a sigh of relief and lifted a hand to push her hair off her face. "Oh, good."

T'arq choked and averted his gaze.

She must look truly awful to get that reaction. "I'll need to wash this goop off and get changed first."

He nodded, still avoiding looking at her. "That would be a good idea. You'll attract far too much attention like that." He flicked his fingers toward her.

She looked down again, the cleaning fluid having molded the fabric to her skin so efficiently that her nipples were as hard as diamonds. She sighed, knowing it was completely useless to fix it.

He shot a glance at her, quickly looking away again. "You look..." he began, but stopped, swallowing the words.

"I look...?"

"Never mind."

She wasn't sure what possessed her to ask, "I want to know what you were going to say. Tell me?"

T'arq's hands clenched and unclenched by his side. His lilac eyes darkened as he took a step closer to her. His tongue darted out to wet his bottom lip, and he swallowed hard before he spoke, his voice deeper than usual. "You are a mess. I want to unwrap you from that hideous uniform and wash every bit of your skin. I want to feel every bit of you with my hands." He was almost growling by the end, his irises now a deep purple and intense in their hue. "I want to taste you."

What? No way did he think that, not with that big strong warrior thing he had going on. Krystal looked up and burst into laughter, head thrown back in mirth.

T'arq blinked. "What?"

She looked at him, so lost and confused, and started laughing again. He huffed and scowled, and still she laughed.

"I'm... sorry..." she gasped for breath, wiping her eyes with her fingers. "This is a joke, right?"

He crossed his arms over his chest and pouted, which set her off again. "What was wrong with what I said?"

Hold on. "You weren't being serious, were you?" Still laughing, she bent and picked the bot up, switching it off and climbing onto her stepstool to put it back on the workbench which was her station. "I'll deal with you tomorrow," she said to the little bot, shaking her finger at it.

She turned back to T'arq, who looked so forlorn that she took pity on him. Did he really not know how cheesy that line was? "It's a little..."

"A little what?"

"Um..." she fiddled with the clasp on her boiler suit, the broken one she had fixed with a cable tie. It was funny how some things were, literally, universal. Duct tape and cable ties appeared to be everywhere.

"I want to know," he said, dropping into a steel chair in the room's corner. He sat back, his big thighs spread wide, the fabric of his shorts pulled tight, and even higher on his thighs —a feat Krystal thought was impossible.

She swallowed, licking her suddenly dry lips. What had he said? Oh, that's right.

"It's just so cheesy," she said, but now she wasn't so sure. Was it really that bad? Or was she just so unused to hearing that kind of thing that she immediately pushed back?

"Cheesy?" he asked, head tilted to one side. "What have dairy products to do with anything?"

"Ah, not cheese. It's a human expression. It means over the top or fake or intense in an overly obvious way."

"You think I'm fake?" he asked, his face smoothing to a carefully blank and unreadable expression.

"I didn't say that." She fiddled with the catch on her uniform again. *Oh, why was this going so wrong?*

"But you think that, don't you?" He crossed his arms over his chest, the sight of his heavily muscled limbs making Krystal's stomach clench.

Get yourself together, woman! Krystal turned around to grip the edge of the workbench.

"Krystal," his voice purred, and she felt an answering pull deep inside her.

"Yes?" She turned back to face him.

"Do you think I'm fake?" His words were quiet, his voice deep and intense.

She sighed. "You won't let this go, will you?"

"No."

How could he make one syllable have so much meaning?

"T'arq, is not that I find you fake exactly, but you do have a reputation."

He muttered under his breath, dropping forward to put his elbows on his knees.

"They have warned me about you. You're kind of..." She shrugged.

His gaze shot to hers, piercing her with their intensity.

She blushed, pulling a face. "You know, someone who sleeps around a lot. Has sex with a lot of different people."

"What's wrong with that?" He looked genuinely confused, and she took pity on him.

"Nothing, if you're being safe and everyone understands what the score is." She shrugged. Not that she was against sexual promiscuity, it was just that in order to feel like wanting to have sex with someone, she had to feel an emotional connection to them.

"Then I don't understand what the problem is."

"Look," she said, dropping to her haunches in front of him. "There's no problem. If you enjoy having sex with lots of people, then that's fine. It's just not me. I can count the number of men I've had sex with on one hand. And Laila knows that, so she warned me from getting involved with you."

His brows drew together. "Because she thinks I would hurt you?"

"Something like that." He looked so downcast that she patted his hand. "Obviously not intentionally, but—"

Her comm unit buzzed. The sound making her pull back from T'arq and, losing her balance, landing on the floor on her backside in front of him. Krystal lifted her wrist to look at the display. It was the chief engineer, not a call she could ignore. She hit the button to answer the call. "Yes?"

"Come to my office. I want to see you."

Krystal gaped. "You want to see me?" Oh god, not now. Not soaked in cleaning fluid and with T'arq here to witness her humiliation.

"Both of you."

Wait. What?

———

B eing in the chief engineer's presence always made Krystal feel slightly uncomfortable, like she'd done something wrong at school and the teacher was about to yell at her. Today it was no different.

She took a deep breath and knocked on the door, then swiped her wrist on the panel to open it. As it opened, she moved to stand just inside the doorway, trying, and failing, to ignore the bulk of T'arq at her back. "You wanted to see me... uh, us?"

"Yes, Krystal. You realize you don't need to knock? If I don't want to be disturbed, the door won't open."

"Yes, I know. It just feels rude to me." Krystal shrugged.

The chief engineer was Taurean, a woman who had to be

the shortest Taurean Krystal had met. That meant nothing compared to Krystal, of course, as Larelle Fe'Law was almost six feet tall. But in a world where the average height was almost seven feet, the woman was short. Unless she was compared with the diminutive Krystal, of course.

Her hair was a dirty blonde, cropped in a no-nonsense style that on Earth would have been called a short back and sides. Her eyes were the same bronze color as her skin, and fine lines radiated from the corners, suggesting she liked to smile.

The chief moved across the small office space to lean against the desk, arms crossed over her chest. The neat uniform would have looked almost perfect, except for the grease stain which spread across one leg. She might be tough and have high expectations, but the chief did not leave all the dirty work to her staff.

Her boss cleared her throat and waved a hand in Krystal's direction.

"Cleaner bot."

"Ahh." She nodded in understanding. "Well, this won't take long. I like your idea for the cloak. It's good."

Krystal beamed. She had listened to the pilots complaining about the existing cloak being temperamental. That they couldn't trust it. It put them on edge. On a whim she had looked up the technical specifications of the cloak and had felt there was something missing. So she had made a proposal that she thought could improve the technology, making it more reliable and improving the pilot's confidence and their performance.

And, if she was truly honest with herself, she listened to the pilots talking in the mess whenever she could because she was always hoping for a small piece of information about T'arq.

Oh, god. She had it bad.

"Yes, it's actually quite an exceptional idea." Larelle looked up from the tablet she was considering. "I want to test it. Could you have the changes ready by this afternoon?"

Krystal was stunned. Her mouth opened and closed. "That soon?" She had only submitted the proposal yesterday after her conversation with Laila.

"Yes, there is a squadron of ships that are out for maintenance right now, so it would be perfect timing. That's why I asked one of the pilots down here to talk it over with you, actually." The chief turned to address T'arq. "Sub-Commander Qu'Ress."

"*You* invited him down here?" Krystal choked. She thought he had been here to check on her. Had she made a complete fool of herself? Again?

Oh, no. No.

Was her ego so big that she thought he, the most gorgeous man she'd ever laid eyes on, would seek her out? While she was covered in muck and wearing what? The universe's most unflattering uniform? Krystal wanted to disappear into the floor.

T'arq nodded. "I take it you want to use my ship to test Krystal's new cloak?"

The chief nodded. "Yes, yours is the only ship not under maintenance right now. Something about already being checked over after... *engine trouble*," she enunciated the words pointedly, one eyebrow raised, "on Irith's Moons."

Krystal tuned out their conversation, instead running some mental calculations. It sounded like they were relying on her. She supposed she could work on the changes. She'd worked out what she needed to do, had even made a test copy. It just needed to be updated on the stealth ship and tested. It should be ready in time.

"I could try to get it ready for this afternoon," she muttered, distantly acknowledging that the chief and T'arq were still talking, but as Krystal pulled out her tablet and began completing calculations, she slid into her own world.

"Would that be all right with you, Krystal?" Larelle asked.

"Huh?" She spun to face her boss. "Sorry, I missed that."

A quirked eyebrow and pursed lips had Krystal blushing and dropping her gaze. She felt a big, warm hand settle on her shoulder.

"Will you have the cloak ready to test on my ship this afternoon?" T'arq asked softly, his breath a whisper against her ear.

"I think so." She tilted her head to one side, considering. "Yes, it will be ready."

"All right, then let's get to it."

"Get to what?"

T'arq's lips twitched, but he kept from smiling. Krystal stared as his tongue darted out to wet his lips.

"You cloaking my ship."

How had he made that seem naughty? She pursed her lips, not wanting to accuse him of flirting while in front of her boss.

Krystal turned to Larelle. "Who will run the testing?"

"You, of course."

"Me? On one of those tiny ships? Out there?" Krystal gaped. It was bad enough that she wasn't on a planet, but was stationed on an actual starship. That had taken some getting used to. But a tiny little stealth ship? Oh no. No way. That would not happen.

T'arq gripped her shoulder in one big, warm but surprisingly gentle hand. "Krystal, I can't test this on my own. I need a flight engineer. And you're the creator of this cloak. If you want it tested, you're going to have to do it."

"But those ships are so small and—"

"Krystal? I need you. Will you do this for me?"

Her heart pounded. What a decision. Could she actually do this?

CHAPTER FIVE

T'arq

He strode into the hangar and headed straight to his stealth ship, still sitting where he had left it. A technician was running through the pre-flight checks, and handed T'arq a tablet as he approached. He began tapping the screens and passing around the ship, going under the belly and between its landing gear to access a maintenance hatch.

T'arq was barely conscious of his movement, borne of regular practice, and his mind wandered. He wasn't sure why he was so nervous. It wasn't as if this was an actual mission. It was just a test flight. Normally he would have found someone to swap with, traded a favor to avoid what would be a mind-numbing few hours. He was used to a lot of action, which was why he was a combat pilot and didn't fly freighters. But the thought of someone else sitting in the cramped cockpit with Krystal? No. Not if he could help it.

I promised Zac I'd look out for her.

He knew that wasn't the entire reason. There had been something vulnerable about Krystal when he had told her he wouldn't do the test flight without her. He paused, hand hovering above the panel in the maintenance hatch, and sighed. T'arq regretted putting her in that position, but he had told the truth. Testing something he did not know how to operate was foolhardy. It was a recipe for disaster. He knew his limits.

But it didn't mean he couldn't sympathize. She was obviously afraid of getting in the small shuttle, but he really did need her on the test flight. He turned his back to the ship and leaned against it, his head falling back to rest against the side of the ship, his eyes closed.

Krystal. Soaked to the skin in some awful smelling cleaning fluid that reminded him of the medical bay. She should not have been so appealing. He grinned. He had been propositioned by courtesans in silk and lace, and none held a candle to Krystal.

He sighed, running his hand through his hair. What he really wanted to know was, did she want him like he wanted her? She had laughed at him. Actually laughed. That had been a blow to his usually quite robust ego.

What did it matter, anyway? She wasn't meant to be his. He'd promised to keep her safe, not get involved with her. Because that would not end well. He was all about having a good time and, although he knew they could have a *fantastic* time together, he would hurt her when he moved on. Because he didn't do relationships. Ever.

He pushed off from the ship with a sigh and reached toward the latch that would engage the ladder for him to climb into the ship. The first time he had seen one of the small stealth ships, it had struck him how strange their appearance was. Their exterior was smooth and rounded, like an elongated egg, and their landing gear gave them the appearance of a bug. Their wings were deceptively strong, holding his weight easily, which was thankful as his preferred way to disembark was through the hatch in the cockpit.

Two points of entry and exit. Every ship had them.

The only issue with the stealth ships was that the crew who flew them had to be very comfortable with each other, as the ships were tiny. Barely big enough for the usual two-person crew, T'arq often flew solo. He really needed a flight engineer, as sometimes even his own skill with the ship was no match for the situations he found himself in. And, if he really wanted to admit his reasoning, one close call was one too many.

The engineer and the pilot sat side by side in the ship, so close that they would brush arms. Currently, T'arq had the ship set for solo flight, with only one chair in the cockpit. That had to be rectified before Krystal could join him on the test flight.

T'arq found a technician, and the two worked quickly to make the changes.. He hoped Krystal liked what he had done. He wanted her to feel comfortable and safe on this test flight. To feel safe and comfortable with him.

An hour later they had finished, T'arq dismissing the tech before doing a last check. He was lying on the floor, his head under the main command console, when a feminine voice squeaked a surprised "Oh!"

T'arq lifted his head, banging it on the underside of the console in his haste. "Fuck!" He rubbed his forehead.

"Oh, no! Are you all right?" Small hands reached to push

his hair back from his face. T'arq blinked to clear his vision and focus.

"What are you doing?"

T'arq was lying on his back, legs bent to fit into the small space in front of the seats. Krystal had climbed over the seat to lie across the armrests, her ass in the air. T'arq groaned as he watched her wriggle to get closer to him.

"Hold still. That was some bang to the head."

"I'm fine," he grumbled, though he lay still while she ran her hands over his face, pressing his skull tightly to test for sore spots. "If it makes you feel better, grab the medi-scanner from that hatch." He pointed to a hatch on the wall with a red cross painted on it.

"Huh. Just like on Earth." Krystal reached across his prone form, straining to reach the hatch. "Why... is... everything... so..." she forced out. Just as her fingers hit the hatch, and it opened with a hiss, she tumbled forward to land on T'arq.

He had been watching her with amusement. Her now clean uniform pulled tightly against her ample breasts as she reached a hand as far as she could, fingers waggling to make her arm long enough to reach the hatch. Somehow, as she had fallen, she had ended up turned away from him, his front pressed to her back and her legs cradled between his own. Her backside— her generous backside—pressed tightly against his groin.

She wriggled to look at him. "I'm so sorry. Did I hurt you?"

Every slight movement she made sent shooting pleasure through him. If she didn't stop moving, she would soon realize the effect she was having on him.

"Stop. Moving." T'arq closed his eyes and willed himself to think of anything else except the curvy woman nestled in his arms. His hands moved of their own accord to frame her waist. He had intended to lift her from him, but instead he groaned and buried his face in her mass of hair, the sweet-smelling curls brushing his face like tender caresses.

So soft. So sweet. So... wriggly?

She stiffened in his arms. "Your... your..." she waved a hand around.

"My what?"

She turned slightly in his arms so she could look up at him. "Your... you know." His lips twitched. "Oh, stop!" She swatted at him, and he captured her wrist with his hand before placing it behind his neck.

Her chest rose and fell rapidly, her breath coming in pants as he trailed his fingers down the inside of her arm to brush lightly against the sides of her rib cage. He skirted the edge of her breast before sliding his hand across her stomach to settle low on her abdomen.

He used his other hand to brush her hair away to expose her neck. "What do I know?" He murmured against her heated skin.

She gasped, dropping her head back on his shoulder, her hand gripping his neck and pulling his head closer to her. He pressed his hand against her abdomen, and she rolled her hips in response.

Oh. This would be one hell of a woman to get to know.

His own hips mimicked hers, the thick hardness of his

cock pushing against the seam of his flight suit, and into the curves of her ass.

He trailed kisses along the side of her neck, turning her head to claim her lips with his. Soft lips opened under his and he drowned in her small moans of pleasure. Her teasing little nips on his lips drove him wild. Scorching heat flooded him and a growl filled the cockpit. It took T'arq a second to realize that he had made the noise.

Shit. What was he doing?

T'arq pulled away, letting his head fall back to the floor and watching as Krystal's dazed, deep brown gaze met his.

"I'm sorry. I should not have done that," he said.

"Oh." She flushed and looked away. She scrambled to get up out of the tight space, elbowing him in the stomach.

He grunted, looking up at her as she scrambled to her feet.

"Here," she said, thrusting the medi-scanner at him as she turned away.

"Thank you." T'arq pulled himself to his feet and flicked the switch on the side of the small, oblong device, turning it on. He ran it over his head, the small pressure headache he had felt beginning, easing.

"Happy now?" he said, handing the device back to Krystal, who stowed it back where it had come from.

On a ship this size, everything had a place. If one thing was out of its home, then chaos would ensue.

She nodded, not looking at him. "I'm sorry," she said, fiddling with a clasp on her uniform. "I shouldn't have..."

"Shouldn't have... what exactly?" He knew he shouldn't press her, but he needed to know.

Her head snapped up to level a glare at him. "I won't lie. I was a willing—"

"Very willing."

She huffed. The noise sounding adorable to T'arq. "All right, I was a *very* willing participant in... that." She waved her hand vaguely toward the floor where their willing participation had occurred.

T'arq was still painfully aroused. Being near Krystal had that effect on him. He adjusted his hard cock in his flight suit to a more comfortable position.

Krystal watched his hands, her pink tongue darting out to wet her lips.

"Very willing," T'arq said again, a teasing grin spreading across his face.

Krystal rolled her eyes at him. "I can't get involved with you."

"I know." His grin flattened. And he *did* know. So why did hearing her say it hurt so much?

"I hate flying." She grimaced.

"I love flying."

"I hate small spaces."

"Small spaces don't worry me," he replied, gesturing with one hand to show the cockpit.

"I don't enjoy feeling trapped."

"Do I make you feel trapped?"

Her head snapped up to look at him. "What? No, of course not."

"Do you trust me?"

She shuffled from one foot to the other, not answering. T'arq's stomach twisted, and he pushed a hand to his abdomen to quell the unease. He forced himself to smile in what he hoped was a reassuring way and sat in the pilot's seat. He patted the flight engineer's chair next to his. Krystal looked from him to the chair and back again, uncertainty written across her face.

"Come on, have a seat. We won't go anywhere until you're confident in my ability to keep you safe. I promise."

Her formerly tense posture eased, and she sat in the chair. "Oh!"

"Do you like it?" He felt warmth spread through him at the look of pleasure on her face.

"You had this made for me, didn't you? How? When?" Her eyes were wide as she looked at him.

It had only been a few hours since their meeting with the chief engineer, but T'arq had been busy. He had pulled in favors and had a custom seat made for the diminutive human. He had noticed the step stool that she carried around when she worked, and that the benches and seats were too high for her to use comfortably.

"If you're going to be effective, you need to be comfortable." He tried to pass it off.

"But it's just one flight. I would have been fine, T'arq," she reached across to pat his hand. Small fingers brushed lightly over his. They had been intimately pressed together, passionately so, and yet this small touch of her hand was so much more than that.

It was a gift.

He cleared his throat and pulled his hand away. No, not going there. He shifted in the seat.

"T'arq?"

"So, the controls for the flight engineer are in the touch panels," he flicked a switch on the armrest of her chair and a panel slid out of a recess in front of them and came to rest within arm's reach. T'arq tapped a series of controls, Krystal watching attentively.

It didn't take long before she was flicking through screens and tapping away as if she had been born knowing how to access these controls.

T'arq settled back and smiled, watching her as she explored.

Krystal looked away from the controls, pushing the panel back into place. She rubbed her arms and sighed, before turning toward him in her seat, a pained expression on her face. "I can't do this."

"What do you mean?"

"I can't go on the test flight with you."

He raised an eyebrow.

She shifted, her fingers tapping a staccato rhythm against the arm of the chair. "It's bad enough being on the Zataras. It took me weeks to get used to it. I hate water, you see."

"Water?" What had water to do with anything?

She sighed, rubbing her temples. "It's not the water, not really. It's the lack of air. Under water or in space. It doesn't matter. There's no air. I'm terrified that I won't be able to breathe out there. That something will happen, and I'll suffocate." Her eyes were filled with tears as she spoke.

T'arq's chest felt tight, like a band was squeezing him and he couldn't do anything to stop it. "Krystal—"

"So, you see. I can't do it. I can't do the test flight. You'll just have to find someone else." The words rushed from her as she scrambled from the seat and rushed from the ship.

CHAPTER SIX

Krystal

Shit. Shit. Shit.

Krystal bolted from the ship, racing past techs and automated hover transports. A horn bleeped at her as she ran in front of a hover transport laden with gear, the automatic braking causing a stack of packages to fall to the hangar floor.

"Sorry!" she shouted, tears streaming down her face as she turned and ran.

It wasn't something she talked about much. Not anymore. But Krystal's fear had solid roots. When Laila had gone to Space Force as a cadet, Krystal had been a child. One evening, her parents had left her with her grandmother while they had gone on a rare evening out. The roads had been wet. A storm had arrived quickly and there had been flash flooding, washing their car from the road and drowning them.

Krystal had dreamed for years that she was stuck in a car, upside down in a river, with no way to get free. She had thought she was mostly over it, but being in space had such a similar feeling for her that the old panic had returned.

She raced through a doorway and into a hall, not caring where she went but knowing she had to get away. She spun. Which way? Where?

And then suddenly his warm arms wrapped around her, and he lifted her from her feet.

"Easy." T'arq's voice rumbled in his chest, and she clung to him like he was a life preserver and she was in fear of drowning.

"Oh god!" she gasped.

"Breathe with me, all right?" His voice was familiar and calming and she focused on his chest, moving up and down, slowly gaining control of her breath.

In and out. Slow and long. One breath. Two breaths. Three. Another.

Her eyes drooped, and she sagged against him. No more fight left in her. "I'm sorry," she whispered against his tear-soaked flight suit.

"Don't apologize," he said, dropping a kiss to the top of her head. "Do you trust me?"

She nodded.

"Your words, Krystal," he said with a not-unkind chuckle.

"Yes, I trust you," she said, and relief flooded her as she realized it was true. She trusted this man with her life. Why? She would think about that later.

"Let's go somewhere quieter, yes?"

She nodded, and he swung her up into his arms. She buried her face into his chest and looped her arms around his neck.

What had she done? She'd kissed him. She'd actually

kissed him. And then he'd shown her the amazing controls, and she'd lost herself in the stealth ship technology. Oh, it was glorious. Everything a nerd would want. And she'd blown it by panicking. So stupid.

A wave of exhaustion pushed through her and she settled deeper into his arms, his chest rumbling with satisfaction.

The rhythm of his steps had almost lulled her into a doze when she heard a door open with the familiar whoosh, and T'arq lowered her gently to her feet. She opened her eyes to find they were in a narrow room. On one wall there were floor to ceiling cupboards with clear fronts displaying a range of supplies. She took a step closer to see everything from field rations to medical supplies and even a selection of weapons. She pulled on the handle of one cupboard that appeared to hold bottles of energy drink; the door beeping at her.

"Access code required," the automated voice scolded her.

"Swipe the chip in your wrist over it. We code each of the doors with an access level, but those are open to everyone." T'arq demonstrated, swiping his hand over a cupboard higher up, which beeped, and a light flashed green before the door sprung open. He reached into the small locker and retrieved a package before shutting the door.

Krystal swiped her own wrist over the cupboard door in front of her, and felt strangely pleased when it flashed green and beeped. The door opened and a blast of cold air reached her, as if she had opened a refrigerator. She reached inside and took a bottle with a pale blue liquid.

"That has a bit of a fruity taste," T'arq said, sitting on a bench that ran the length of the opposite wall. He sprawled out with his legs stretched in front of him and his hands folded behind his head. "I'm not sure if it's to the human palate, but try it." He nodded in reassurance.

"What is this place?" Krystal asked, sitting down next to him, keeping a little distance between them on the bench. She brushed her fingers over the padded bench, the fabric feeling like some kind of micro suede, so soft.

"It's a resupply room. If you get off a shuttle and need to get back out again but don't have time to put in a requisition from the main store, then you can get most of what you need here."

"Oh. Why not use the replicators?"

"Takes too much energy, and too much time. It's much easier and more efficient to have a steady supply on hand. We can replicate anything unusual on request." He pointed to the small replicator unit at the end of the room.

"That makes sense." Krystal opened the bottle of liquid and took a tentative sip. Flavor exploded on her taste buds. T'arq was right. It was fruity—like a mix of pineapple and kiwi fruit. She made a noise of approval and took a bigger swallow.

He grinned and stretched his arms out along the back of the bench, letting his head drop back. He breathed in deeply.

Krystal watched as his features relaxed. She turned toward him, tucking her feet underneath her so they didn't dangle above the ground like a child's. That was the problem with everything on the Zataras; they made it for giants.

Except the flight engineer's chair. That was customized to fit her. That was a lot of trouble to go to for one test flight. But why?

"What do you want from me, T'arq?"

"Hmm?" He opened one eye and peered at her without moving his head.

"I need to know what you want."

He shifted slowly, turning toward her. One leg hitched on the bench and his arm stretched out behind her. Head tilted to one side; his eyes traveled over her face. Krystal sat in silence, waiting for the answer. She had a short fuse, but she also knew when to be patient. And getting this answer from him needed patience in buckets.

"I don't think I know," he finally said. The words were soft, his eyes on hers as his fingers tapped idly on the back of the bench.

"I know what I want," she said, taking another swig from the bottle. "I want to save lives. And my cloak will save lives."

"But...?"

She sighed, slumping. "But I can't do the testing. Not out there." She gestured toward the direction of the hangar, her skin paling slightly, and she swallowed hard.

"Why not?"

She looked at him with incredulity. "Are you blind?"

He laughed.

"You saw what just happened! That was just me sitting in the cockpit safely on a starship. Imagine what it's going to be like when I can't get off the damned thing." She dropped her head into her hands and groaned. "It's bad enough that I panicked. What if I completely screw up the testing?" She wailed.

"Then we'll do it until we get it right." He reached out and peeled one of her hands away to hold it in his own. He squeezed gently, forcing Krystal to look at him.

"We... we will?" she asked, eyes wide.

"We'll go back to the stealth ship and we'll try again. We'll test it until you get it right." He smiled gently and smoothed his thumb back and forth over her hand. The long strokes calming her racing pulse. She took a shaky breath and released it, tension seeping from her.

"Oh." The matter-of-fact way that he delivered the statement floored her. Just like that. She wasn't a problem, an issue to solve. Her anxiety wasn't being treated as a major hurdle. "Together?"

He reached out with his other hand to squeeze her shoulder gently. "Together."

———

As the big Taurean slid into the pilot's seat, Krystal admired how sinuously he moved. He knew where everything was on this small ship. Now that she was a little calmer, she had spent some time alongside T'arq checking every nook and cranny on the ship, so she was familiar with it. He reasoned she would feel safer if she knew the ship better.

Krystal had laughed and accused him of likening the ship to a person.

"Respect your tools, Krystal. That's what every good engineer does, right?"

She had nodded and realized he was correct. The ship was a tool, a tool she needed to use to meet her objective. It wasn't an obstacle in the way; it was the way.

With that change in attitude, she found the task a lot easier, even if she wasn't entirely comfortable yet.

"Ready?" T'arq asked her, gesturing for her to take the flight engineer's seat.

"No."

"All right, then we won't go." He unbuckled the straps holding him safely in the seat.

"Wait," she said, holding up a hand to stay his movements. "Can I just have a minute?"

"Take as long as you need," he said, settling back in his chair.

Krystal took some long breaths, counting backwards from ten in her head, trying to locate things she could sense with her senses, all those tools she had learned to help with her anxiety. Gradually, her tense shoulders loosened and her heart rate steadied.

"OK. I'm good." She scrambled into the smaller seat next to T'arq, brushing against him as she reached to fasten herself into the seat with the straps he had shown her how to use.

"May I?" he asked, gesturing at the straps.

"Yes."

He worked the straps tighter around her. Over her shoulders. Across her chest, squashing her breasts uncomfortably, around her waist, and over her thighs. Her lower legs could move freely, as could her arms, but her torso was strapped solidly into the seat.

"All right?" he asked.

"Yes."

He smiled reassuringly. "I'm going to talk to you while I go through the pre-flight sequence, so you know what I'm doing. If you want me to stop at any point, let me know."

"OK." That sounded fine. She focused on T'arq's voice,

the deep tones soothing her frayed nerves as he ran through the sequence of checks before their craft would be ready for the test flight.

"T'arq?"

"Yes, little mouse?" He shot a grin at her, his lilac eyes warm, fine lines crinkling at the corners. His hands still worked the screens in front of him with the ease of oft-repeated patterns.

"Nothing bad is going to happen to us, is it?"

She hated she felt she had to ask.

"Of course not. I'll keep you safe. It's just a test flight. We'll go out as far as we need to make sure the cloak works like you want it to."

She breathed out in a rush. "And if I want to come back?"

"We'll turn right back." He held her gaze until she nodded and smiled a small, nervous smile.

"All right. I just need to check that I've uploaded everything, and then we can go."

T'arq nodded and continued his checks, the sound of his voice filling the cockpit.

"Now for the cockpit hatch. Ready?"

Krystal forced her shoulders to relax. "Yes."

A mechanical whirring sounded as the hatch slid into place, not unlike a jet fighter that she had seen in an old movie. They were now enclosed in the small cockpit; the hatch rising from waist height to continue over their heads.

"It's designed to allow for visual confirmation. They used to have view screens only, but pilots like to use their senses, even if they don't work as well as the displays."

He passed her a headset, and tapped the right side of the headset near her ear, a small display screen emerging to slide over one eye. She struggled to focus on it, one eye looking out of the cockpit window and the other on the translucent display. She blinked, her vision finally clearing to see streams of data flashing before her eyes.

"Whoa!" She swallowed, fighting nausea. Her hands gripped the armrests tightly, fighting the need to rip the headset off.

"Sorry," T'arq said, his hand touching her headset and brushing her hair as his fingers moved over the earpiece. He smoothed his hand over her hair. "I've changed the settings, so it should be better. Open your eyes and give it another try, OK?"

She nodded, tentatively obeying.

"Is that better?" he asked.

Thankfully, the stream of information flooding her vision had reduced significantly. She nodded. "Yes, much better. How do you stand it? I almost wanted to vomit."

He chuckled. "It comes with practice. There was a time when pilots had neural interfaces to assist with parsing that much information, turning us into walking computers."

"Really? Nobody mentioned that." She was immediately curious, turning in her seat to face T'arq, who pulled his hand away and put on his own headset.

He shrugged. "We don't talk about it. It wasn't a... great time in Taurean history. It took them a few disasters before they realized pilots needed to be more man—or woman— than machine." He flicked a few more switches, and the engines hummed.

A voice filled the cockpit. "Stealth Ship Qu'Ress Alpha. You are good for departure. Good luck, Sub-Commander."

"Thank you, but we don't need luck. We have a new cloak." He winked at Krystal.

Oh, dear lord. She was about to shoot into space in the company of a playboy sexpot in something that looked like a giant suppository.

What was she thinking?

She didn't realize she was scrabbling for the latch on the harness until a large, warm hand landed on her thigh. His hands were huge. His pinky finger wrapped around one side of her thigh, and his thumb on the other side. He kneaded her tense muscles gently and hummed.

She closed her eyes and focused on slowing her breathing.

What on... was that welcome to the jungle? No way!

"What are you humming?" she asked.

How did he know one of her favorite songs?

He grinned and kept humming, not looking at her.

"Where did you learn that?" She tilted her head to one side and began humming along with him before breaking out in the chorus, her fingers drumming the beat on the armrests of her seat. She closed her eyes and sang, her heart lighter than it had been in days. When she was finished, she collapsed with laughter.

"You hum when you're nervous, you know." T'arq turned to her with a wink.

"Really? I know I sing when I work. I didn't realize that I did it when I was nervous as well." She gave a little frown of concentration. "Where did you learn that song?"

T'arq just grinned and gunned the engine.

CHAPTER SEVEN

T'arq

It had worked. He had distracted Krystal long enough that she hadn't even noticed that they were no longer in the hangar.

She gasped in surprise as they steadily moved away from the Zataras. The bulk of the large starship was visible through the glass of the cockpit as T'arq slowly turned the stealth ship so Krystal could take in the view.

The starship was a rough rectangular prism, with huge guns mounted at regular intervals in recesses along the dull silver hull. There were windows for the crew to use, but these were smaller than those on pleasure craft. By necessity, the Zataras was designed to withstand a significant attack, and that meant looks were not the primary concern in its design.

He wondered what she would make of one of the Taurean pleasure liners, large cruise starships designed for recreation. She'd like it, he decided. As long as she got to talk to the designers and engineers so she could see how everything worked. He smiled at the thought.

As they slowly drifted past, the starship's name came into view, painted in letters on the hull three times the size of their shuttle.

Krystal gaped, turning to exclaim, "I've never seen it like this. It's huge!"

He sniggered.

"You would make a joke out of that." She crossed her arms, or at least tried to, but the straps of her harness made her movements jerky and she gave up with a huff.

"I'm just relieved that you're doing well."

She nodded slowly. "Yeah, it's actually OK. I'm not sure what I was expecting, but I built it up in my mind to be something awful and..."

"It's beautiful out here, isn't it?" He gestured at the expanse of space that emerged as they slowly drifted past the Zataras' many windows.

"Yes," she said absently, taking in the view, almost overwhelming in its vastness.

T'arq rarely shared this part of his life with someone, at least for their first time. Seeing the rapt attention Krystal was dedicating to the vista started a warmth spreading through his chest.

"You're in charge. What now?" he asked Krystal.

She shot him a sharp look. "You know we have a flight path. Let's stick to that. And I'm so far from being in control of this, it's not funny."

"Easy. Just trying to make you feel more comfortable."

She mumbled something under her breath, and his lips twitched. She was adorable when she got like this.

"I am not adorable. I might be short, but I'm fierce."

"You can read my thoughts?"

"No, but you just confirmed what you were thinking, didn't you?"

He laughed. "Little mouse, you are ferocious. Remind me never to cross you."

She nodded and gave a satisfied grunt. T'arq struggled not to grin.

"So our flight plan has us heading on a pretty straightforward path to that asteroid field." T'arq flicked the screen in the middle of the display so Krystal could see, placing a marker for the Zataras.

"That seems an awfully long way from the ship." Krystal's voice hitched at the end, and T'arq felt a rush of sympathy. She really had pushed her boundaries to set foot on the stealth ship, let alone go so far away from the safety of the large starship.

"It's pretty close when you consider how fast these little gems can go," he said, patting the cockpit wall nearest him affectionately.

"I'm not sure..."

T'arq pulled the ship in to hover near the Zataras, using the greater bulk of the big starship to anchor them. He unclipped his harness and turned in his seat to face Krystal.

"Oh, my god! Strap yourself back in!" She grabbed at him frantically.

"Hey, hey. It's fine." He reached over to stay her hands, that were flailing around in panic. She grabbed his hands so tightly he thought she might cut the circulation off.

She grumbled something under her breath, and he lifted an eyebrow.

She huffed reluctantly. "Just stop being reckless!"

"Undoing my harness is not reckless. We're tethered to the Zataras and we're not going anywhere. I often have to move to the back of the ship." He gestured with his head behind them to the small cargo hold, barely big enough for him to stand and certainly not big enough for him to stretch his arms out.

"Why?" She looked where he was gesturing, eyebrows drawn together in a frown.

"It's where the galley is." His words were even as if he were calming a frightened animal.

She took several breaths, trying to calm herself. "I suppose on the longer trips, you have to eat. And I hate those awful ration bars." They shared a smile. The Taurean ration bars were a necessity on missions, but the flavor left a lot to be desired.

"You need your data."

She nodded, still gripping his hands tightly.

"And you want to get back to the Zataras quickly?"

She nodded again, this time releasing his hands and flexing her fingers.

"So, shall we get to it?"

She took a deep breath and sighed, appearing to brace herself mentally. "Yes. Let's do this."

———

Three hours later and T'arq was bored out of his mind. When Krystal focused, she really focused. She barely even grunted at him as she stared at the screens in front of her, flipping through them rapidly. The contrast between this Krystal and when she was panicked was massive.

T'arq had made three cups of coffee, had checked over every possible gauge and setting—twice—and was thinking that counting the rivets in the hull would be an entertaining task. His butt felt like it was chair shaped, and he shifted in his seat, warranting a warning huff from the small woman in the seat next to him.

"Krystal?" he asked, not for the first time.

She tapped on the screen and, just when he thought she wouldn't reply, she did. "Hmm?"

"How much longer?" He had held out as long as he could. The rivets could wait a little longer.

There was another long pause as she continued tapping on the screen, a line drawn between her brows showing her concentration.

T'arq counted under his breath. *Three... two... one—*

"I need to test the cloak when we use the comm. That was an issue with the last cloak, right?"

T'arq grimaced. It *was* the major flaw. The cloak worked, but would fail as soon as a communication was sent or received, which meant that the cloak could fail at any moment and calling for help would be a disaster.

"Yes, that was a problem. How do you want to test it?"

Krystal tapped on her screen, a crease between her brows. It took her so long to reply that T'arq was thinking that she hadn't heard him.

"Let's contact the Zataras and see if it works."

T'arq nodded, reaching for his comm, relieved to have something to do. He had resorted to counting the number of times Krystal rubbed her temples, which she apparently did when deep in thought. Twelve. She had rubbed her temples twelve times since he had counted.

He keyed the comm. "Zataras, this is Stealth Ship Qu'Ress Alpha."

"Qu'Ress Alpha, what can I do for you?"

"Just running some testing. Can you keep the comm open for a few minutes?"

"Absolutely."

Krystal tapped away on her screen, streams of data rolling past so fast that T'arq had no hope of understanding what was going on. Without the training, how was she taking it all in?

T'arq muted the comm. "Krystal?"

"Just a minute," she said, waving a hand dismissively.

He smiled. So much for being anxious and overwhelmed. Once her brain was engaged, she was so preoccupied that it didn't matter what else was going on.

The sounds of the bridge on the Zataras rolled over the speaker, the distant voices chattering softly in the background and the familiar electronic noises of a battleship bridge rolling over T'arq. He had once thought to pilot a starship like the Zataras, but then he had met Zac at the military academy on Taurus and everything had changed. Zac, a son of an elite Taurean family with a military pedigree T'arq could only dream about, had taken him under his wing. The two had quickly become friends, almost inseparable. So much so that when it became known that T'arq had no preference for gender in his partners, many suggested that they were lovers. But no. T'arq loved Zac, but like a brother, nothing more.

And when Laila arrived on the scene? T'arq could see

how happy she made Zac, and how could he begrudge his closest friend such happiness?

But in the quiet hours of the morning, lying alone in his bed, he ached for more.

Krystal's voice shook him from his thoughts. "I'm going to test the cloak now. I have enough baseline data."

"You mean you haven't been testing the cloak?"

What had she been doing for three hours?

She shot him a puzzled look. "Of course not. I needed control data."

T'arq groaned, letting his head fall back against the headrest.

"T'arq?"

He rolled his head on the headrest to look at her. "Yes?"

Krystal glanced from him to her tablet. "We need to engage the cloak, but..." she trailed off and bit her bottom lip.

T'arq watched as she chewed on it between neat, white teeth, making her lip redden. He swallowed, forcing himself to look away.

"Go on," he said, picking up a tablet and mindlessly flipping through the screens to stop staring at Krystal's lips.

Get a hold of yourself!

"I need to see if the Zataras can see us on their scans when the cloak is up," she paused and then finished in a rush, "but I'm worried it's going to fail, and I'll look like an idiot and you'll be angry because we've been out here for hours."

She looked like she was about to cry and T'arq couldn't have stopped himself from consoling her if he tried. He reached over with one large callused hand and cupped her face, brushing his thumb down her cheek.

"It's not a waste of time. I believe in you and your work. I'm sorry I've been grumpy. I've enjoyed this time spent with you. Really." He said, the truth of the words bringing a warm glow to his chest and a reassuring smile.

She nodded and swiped at her eyes with the back of her fingers. "You're sure?"

"Absolutely."

She took a shaky breath. "Ok. Then I'm going to engage the cloak. Can you have the Zataras see if they notice anything?"

He nodded, picking up the comm and hailing the big starship. "Zataras?"

"Here, Qu'Ress Alpha."

Krystal's fingers moved so fast on the screen that he couldn't tell what she was pressing. She made one last, definitive gesture on the screen and then said, her voice steady, "The cloak is engaged."

"Check your scans," T'arq directed., "are we appearing?"

After a long moment of silence, a stunned voice came over the comm. "No... I assume this is what you were expecting?"

T'arq and Krystal grinned. She punched her fist in the air in celebration and T'arq laughed.

"Has it worked, Qu'Ress?" This time it was the voice of Captain Tomas Fa'Rell, the deep tones unmistakable over the comm.

T'arq looked to Krystal, gesturing to the comm. She hesitantly flicked her mic and spoke. "Initial testing appears positive, sir."

They heard excited whoops in the background. T'arq imagined the news would be quite good for the bridge crew, who had witnessed many a pilot's death in battle. One more step to keeping them safer was not to be glossed over.

"Although," Krystal continued, "I'd like to see it working with physical interference."

T'arq spoke up, "Permission to alter our flight plan, Zataras?"

"Granted. Just be careful. We can't track you anymore, Qu'Ress."

"Noted. Qu'Ress out."

Communication with the Zataras now cut, T'arq let out a whoop that had Krystal jump in her seat. She pressed a hand to her chest and glanced at T'arq, who grinned at her.

"Do you realize what you have done?"

Her brows drew together as she shook her head slightly.

"You've saved hundreds, maybe even thousands of lives! Krystal, you've done it!" His enthusiasm was contagious, and a small smile broke out across her face.

"So far it's looking good, yes."

"Oh, don't be a pessimist. It's working and will continue to work. I know you can do it." T'arq turned back to the controls and flicked a few screens to find a suitable obstacle to test the cloak. The asteroid field they had been heading toward should do nicely. He re-charted the course to go near the field, planning to guide the ship manually once they arrived.

"It's going to be awhile until we get to the asteroid field. Are you hungry?"

A growl from Krystal's stomach greeted his question, and she flushed.

"I'll take that as a yes."

Until now, the ship had not used the artificial gravity. With T'arq and Krystal strapped into their seats and everything stowed in its place, there was no need. But T'arq did not like preparing food in zero gravity. It could get messy easily, and liquids were not friendly to electronics.

He unstrapped himself from the seat and eased himself upright, stretching as much as the small space allowed. Once upon a time, being strapped into a seat for hours on end didn't cause him any grief. Age found everyone, he supposed. If you were lucky.

Chuckling to himself, he paused, realizing Krystal was staring at him, mouth open.

"What?"

"Nothing," she mumbled, face red and her head down, the dark curls falling forward to hide her face from him.

He looked at her for a long moment, but she studiously refused to look up, so he shrugged and made his way into the tiny galley cum cargo hold. Stealth ships were primarily used in combat for quick dash and fire missions. The cargo hold was really a multi-purpose space, with a pull-out hygiene station that T'arq tried to only use in a pinch, and a small food preparation area housed in a cupboard. There were tie-down rings to hold boxes, though the space was empty right now.

He began pulling out the various packets and a container to make their meal. With a practiced flick of the wrist, the heating element in a silver package activated. He put it aside as he flicked through the rest of the stash of ready meals until he found what he was looking for.

"Hah! There you are," he muttered, quickly setting this one to heating as well.

In a few short minutes, he had arranged their food on a tray. He made his way back into the main cabin with it and, with a command to the on-board computer, a small tabletop slid from a recessed panel to click into place between the two chairs.

"Here," T'arq said as he slid into his seat. "Eat."

"In a minute," Krystal replied, head still bowed and busily tapping away on her tablet.

"No. Now, little mouse. You need your energy if you're to be of any use."

She glanced up at him and, with a resigned twist of her lips, she nodded. "Can I undo the harness?"

"Of course," T'arq said. "Do you need some help?" He winked, trying for his most playful grin. He must have succeeded because she barked out a laugh in reply, quickly undoing the straps so she could turn in the seat and appraise the food.

"What is it?" she asked, pointing at one of the silver packages, steam rising from the top.

"Just a few things I thought you might like." Why was he so concerned? She was sensible. If she was hungry, then she would eat. "There's a spiced Taurean stew, but I wasn't sure if you'd like it, so I also have an Earth dish that the computer said was popular with humans." He pushed the second silver package to her and offered her a fork.

She pulled the package toward her side of the tray and gave a tentative sniff, then looked into the package. Incredulously, she exclaimed, "Tom Yum noodle soup? You have to be kidding me!"

Thankful that he had been around enough humans to understand their expressions, he laughed. "Do you like it then?"

Krystal had already shoved a mouthful of the dish into

her mouth, so she swallowed and choked out, "It's one of my favorites. Thank you."

That warm feeling spread through T'arq again. Pushing it aside, he focused on eating. He'd found her intriguing from the first, but seeing these different sides of her made him like her even more.

Krystal's tablet beeped and with one hand busy with her food, she swiped at the screen with the other.

T'arq paused, fork halfway to his mouth, and turned his head in time to see Krystal's grip on the container slip. A rain of noodles and hot liquid sprayed across the tablet and into her lap.

"Shit!"

He moved quickly, lifting her bodily from the chair and stripping her flight suit and boots from her, so she stood in front of him, clad only in her underwear. He ran his hands over her, grabbing the medi-scanner and scanning her red skin with the wand.

She was shaking by the time he was done. "T'arq?"

He looked up at her from where he was running the medi-scanner over her feet, straightening to kneel with his head level with hers. "What's wrong?" T'arq reached out to grasp her upper arms in his hands, kneading gently.

Big brown eyes filled with tears. "Please tell me all my data isn't gone?"

CHAPTER EIGHT

Krystal

Every worst-case scenario ran through Krystal's head. Had she deleted all the data? Had the soup—of all things—damaged the tablet irreparably and she would have to pay for it out of her wages? What about the ship? How stupid could she be?

She clutched at her chest, her breath coming in sharp pants.

Oh no. This could not be happening. Not here, not now.

She had been running the new cloak alongside the main AI for the ship, not wanting to change its programming without knowing the impact. That meant it only housed the program on the tablet. That was now covered in soup.

"Can you pass me the tablet?" She forced the words out, her voice hoarse.

T'arq reached across and, wiping a stray noodle from the screen, passed it to her. "It's not damaged. These things can handle a beating." He smiled.

She gaped at him as she blotted liquid from the screen with a cloth he handed her.

"See?" He leaned in a tapped a button, the screen coming to life. "We made these things able to handle hard use. A little soup wouldn't hurt it."

Krystal felt her chest ease and her knees wobble in relief. She sat heavily on her seat, flicking quickly through the tablet to make sure what T'arq had said was true. Then she checked again, just to make sure.

A broad smile split her face as she realized he was right. She hadn't lost anything. She jumped to her feet and gave a little happy dance, putting the tablet safely on her seat first. Hands in the air, she closed her eyes and hopped on the spot.

An icy blast of air from the ship's climate control hit her bare skin and Krystal froze, eyes wide as she looked down at herself. She was dancing around in her underwear and socks on a spaceship with a giant alien—a giant, extremely attractive alien—who was looking at her like he wanted to eat her.

And she was wearing panties with cartoon cats on. Great. She blushed.

T'arq blinked, breaking whatever spell had him frozen to the spot, and cleared his throat.

She shivered and wrapped her arms around her midsection. "It's probably a long shot, but is there something else I can wear?" She poked with one foot at the crumpled mess of soup-soaked clothing on the floor.

"Not that will fit you, but I might be able to replicate something." He reached above her head to open a hatch; his chest tantalizingly close. She breathed in deeply, the spicy scent of his skin, and whatever soap he used surrounding her.

He pulled something from the hatch and took a step back, snapping the small compartment shut with one big hand. "Here," he said, shaking open a thin blanket and wrapping it around her shoulders.

Krystal tugged the ends together across her chest, surprised at how warm the lightweight fabric was. "Thank you."

He grinned wolfishly. "Though I think I like the small felines better," he said, lifting one eyebrow and winking at her.

Krystal ducked her head, avoiding his gaze. Would she ever not be an accident-prone mess around him? She sighed, looking up to see T'arq disappear through the door to the cargo bay, which slid open at his approach.

She wrapped the blanket tighter around herself and shivered, shifting from foot to foot. The cold temperature of space was no joke, and this stealth ship was freezing now that she didn't have the furnace of T'arq standing next to her, the cold soaking through even the thick socks on her feet.

Seriously, how did he run so hot? It was inhuman. Of course it was inhuman. He was an *alien*. She curled up on her chair, feet tucked underneath her, and stared out the cockpit window and pulled the tablet onto her lap. Soon she was involved with her work once more.

"Krystal?" T'arq stuck his head out of the doorway some minutes later.

She climbed out of the chair and faced him. "Yes?"

"Here you go," T'arq said, joining her in the cockpit with a flourish of fabric. "All done." He smiled expectantly and watched her as if waiting for a reaction.

Vulnerable as she felt, she had to admit that he was doing

a lot to help her feel comfortable, despite how cold her socked feet felt against the metal grille of the floor.

"What...?" Krystal stared at the deep purple-colored bundle in his arms.

T'arq looked down, then back up at her. "It's your new flight suit. What do you think?"

"It's purple." She reached out and ran her hands over the soft fabric.

He smiled smugly as he watched her reverently touch his offering. "Yes. Your favorite color."

She blinked at him. "How...?"

He handed her the bundle, but when she stood there with it in her hands, gaping at him, he took it back. He kneeled before her again and opened the zipper at the front, holding it so she could step into it. She braced herself on his shoulders as she did so, first one leg, then the other. He slid the fabric up her legs, his warm knuckles brushing against her skin as he did so. She shivered.

"I forget you run colder than us Taureans. I'll turn up the heat."

She didn't correct him, fighting to not gasp as he tugged the suit over her backside and held it open for her to pull it up her arms.

He reached for the zipper, but Krystal decided that enough was enough and she batted his hand away from her crotch where the tag waited, ready to be tugged closed. That was one place she doubted she would survive should he touch her there.

This. Was. Torture.

Krystal barely avoided getting her hair trapped in the zipper, flicking it over her shoulder at the last minute. The suit fit her like a second skin. None of those oversized uniforms that she had been wearing.

"It's tight."

"Nonsense. It fits perfectly."

She looked down at herself dubiously, worried that the suit would burst at the seams if she bent over. She moved tentatively, surprised when the suit moved with her. The fabric was sturdy, but stretchy. She dropped into a crouch. No tearing. She swung her arms overhead. No tearing. She kicked and spun. No tearing.

Amazing.

Breathless, she caught T'arq staring at her, an amused grin on his face.

She cleared her throat. "Let's get back to it then." She slid back into her seat, T'arq having wiped the console and their seats of any remnant soup.

"Closed containers for you from now on," he said, handing her a cup with a straw, not unlike a toddler's sip cup.

She took it and sipped, pleased when a fruity flavor, like a cross between mango and orange, filled her mouth. "Juice?"

He nodded. "From the Darnae tree. It's native to my planet."

"You're not from Taurus?"

He hesitated before answering. "No... not originally." There was something in his tone that suggested to Krystal to not push further. The short answer stopping any further questioning.

Krystal picked up her tablet. "To the asteroid field?"

"Heading there right now."

They made good time, reaching the asteroid field with enough time for Krystal to collect the data she needed before beginning the cloak testing with physical obstacles interfering.

"Why do you need to test the cloak like this?" T'arq asked.

Busily watching the displays of data, and occasionally altering something by tapping on the screen, Krystal answered him absently. "It's easy enough to cloak a ship in the distance. It's another thing entirely to hide a ship that's close. If something triggers a sensor and they scan..."

T'arq finished the sentence for her. "... then all they need to do is watch for a flicker and change in the scenery and the cloak is useless."

"Pretty much."

"And the comm?"

A beeping distracted her, tapping and adjusting settings until the noise stopped.

"The same thing, really. Light and sound are both waves, and if they interfere with each other, then they can disrupt the image."

He nodded.

"I want to make sure there is no chance of disruption ever happening again."

Krystal had heard horror stories of entire squadrons of ships being lost because of previous cloaks failing at exactly the wrong time. She shuddered. She didn't want any blood on her hands.

"Are you cold? I can turn the heat up."

"No, I'm fine."

Far from what she had expected, spending this much

time with him in such close quarters had her feeling a little ashamed at the assumptions she'd made about him. She should apologize.

"T'arq?"

He turned to face her, his full attention on her, and she found herself a little overwhelmed at the intensity of his gaze. Those purple eyes glowed, and she struggled to keep her thoughts straight. What would it be like to have his attention all the time? To be his one and only?

She chickened out.

"Ah, let's try the cloak in the asteroid field."

His eyes crinkled at the corners, but he did not smile. It was as if he knew she had wanted to say something else and had been too scared. He didn't push her though, and instead just quirked an eyebrow before turning to the controls and easing the ship close to a large asteroid.

"Is this OK?" He gestured to the giant rock, over ten times the size of the ship, and she nodded.

The next hour flew as Krystal deployed external sensors to test the cloak's performance from outside the ship. They tried slow flybys, gradually increasing in speed until Krystal was satisfied that the ship's cloak would replicate the exterior of an object it passed in front of.

"It's working!" She exclaimed, excitement pulsing through her. She reached out and grabbed T'arq's hand, squeezing before she realized what she was doing.

"What's next?" he asked.

She let go of his hand. "We need to contact the Zataras again and see if the combination of objects and comm signal has any effect on the cloak."

"OK, I'll do that."

T'arq keyed the comm. "Huh. That's strange."

Krystal watched as T'arq's previously calm manner became much more serious. His hands moved over the various controls much faster than he had since they'd boarded the stealth ship,

"Starship Zataras, this is Qu'Ress Alpha."

Silence.

"We need to move the ship to get a better signal," T'arq said as he moved the ship away from the asteroid where it had been tethered while they finished the testing.

Krystal realized he had been humoring her. Keeping calm and fluid movements to not startle her. The speed at which he maneuvered the ship made her stomach jump. She swallowed past a lump in her throat and must have made a noise because T'arq's hand reached out to pat hers where it was gripping the armrest of her chair, knuckles white.

"Sorry. I need to get us back in range... quickly."

Krystal nodded and closed her eyes, fighting the impending sense of doom that had flooded her.

Breathe in, one... two... and out... one... two. The mantra running through her head helped her heart rate to slow somewhat, though it still pounded in her chest.

She looked at T'arq as he guided the ship so smoothly, his hands moving sinuously over the controls, like he was playing a musical instrument. Muscle memory knew where every small switch was, where every tap of a finger would show information on the display.

"Let's try here." T'arq's voice was strained.

They had quickly popped out of the bulk of the asteroid belt and, as Krystal confirmed with her own map, they should now have an unobstructed comm path to the starship.

They still knew where they were and there was no issue with making it back to the Zataras.

T'arq tried to raise the Zataras on comms again, but there was still no answer.

"Please tell me that there's a simple reason we can't reach them?" Krystal pleaded.

T'arq set an automation to continue trying to raise the Zataras.

"There are a couple of potential reasons," T'arq began slowly, his purple eyes behind the display screen of his headset eerily multi-hued. He had never looked more alien to her than he did right now.

"And they are?" She glanced at her hands gripping the armrest, moving her fingers to ease the stiffness. How long had she been gripping the armrest?

"They could be doing maintenance."

"No. I know that maintenance schedule inside out. There's no maintenance being conducted right now."

T'arq nodded. "It could be a solar storm interfering with the signal."

Krystal scanned the area between them and the Zataras' last known position. "Nope. No solar storms."

"Our comms could be down."

"They're not. I checked."

T'arq stared out the window across the broad expanse of the asteroid field. "That leaves one option, and you will not like it."

Krystal felt the blood rush from her face. "No."

"I'm sorry."

"You can't be serious."

T'arq didn't respond. The silence spreading between them like some ominous cloud.

"See that?" T'arq tilted his screen toward her so she could see the object he had magnified. It looked like an electronic spider in a web. The dull black material was barely distinguishable on the backdrop of space, but T'arq had spotted it.

"What is it?"

Her heart was hammering so loudly she could hear rushing. The still silence of the cockpit took on an ominous edge as they stared at the strange construction.

T'arq turned to meet her eyes. "It's a Xakul comm signal jammer."

Krystal gaped at him. *No. Oh no.*

It was bad enough that they were in actual space, away from the safety of the large starship. She had focused on her work and pushed that thought aside, which was no minor achievement.

But this?

The Xakul were formidable opponents, taller even than a Taurean warrior when they stood on the rear two of their six legs. She had heard stories of how fast they could run, and it was terrifying. There were rumors about one Xakul soldier who had escaped confinement on a Space Force base on Earth... and if even half of what Krystal had heard was true, then she never wanted to see one in person.

"Are you telling me I am in a ship the size of a shoebox, in the middle of some unmapped asteroid field, with no way to contact the Zataras," a hard edge entered her voice, "and there are goddamned Xakul nearby?"

CHAPTER NINE

T'arq

As the color drained from Krystal's face, T'arq felt a rush of sympathy. He would take her back to the Zataras if he could, but time was critical. Nobody just stumbled across the Xakul like this. He had to find out what they were doing out here.

"Yes. That's exactly what I'm telling you. And we can't just leave. I have to find out why they are here and what they are planning."

He didn't have a good feeling about this, especially since they were so close to Earth's solar system. Only a half day at maximum speed for the Zataras. And there were Xakul ships who could match that pace. Their presence here could only mean bad news for Earth.

T'arq hoped he was wrong.

He glanced at the woman sitting next to him. She looked so small and helpless; her hands twisted together anxiously.

Maybe if he... he pushed a few controls and music flowed into the cockpit.

"Is that—"

"Yes. Greatest rock hits of the 1990s. I found the album in the data banks on the Zataras."

"What?" Krystal's eyes were enormous as she stared at him.

"I thought it might help you feel calmer?"

"Listening to music from the late 20th century as we fly around an asteroid field in a glorified tin can?"

T'arq didn't take offense. He knew she was finding this difficult, so he just nodded.

"I suppose this is just another day at the office for you," she muttered.

T'arq moved the ship closer to the dark mass of the signal jammer.

"Dear lord, it's huge!" Krystal breathed as they approached.

T'arq had set up proximity alerts to warn them if any Xakul came within visual range, and relaxed slightly when nothing sounded. He drifted the ship closer to the jammer, which loomed easily ten times the size of their stealth ship.

It resembled a spider's web, each quadrant spreading out from a central hub where the bulk of the jamming equipment was housed.

"They have switched it on since we arrived, right?" Krystal asked.

"Yes, otherwise we couldn't have reached the Zataras at all."

"So that means the Xakul are very close."

"Unless they can operate it from long distances, but..."

"You find that unlikely."

"Exactly."

They were silent for long moments as T'arq scanned the signal jammer for any information they could get. This would be very useful to the intelligence corps, he suspected.

"Have you seen one of these before?" she asked, gesturing at the expanse of Xakul tech spread out in front of them.

"Not this size. Much smaller."

"Oh."

The few times T'arq had run across this kind of technology had been when he was working solo, and the signal jammers were much, much smaller. No larger than a meter across. That they had increased the size of them to such a degree, and without the Taurean military knowing? That was alarming.

He slowly raised the ship until they were level with the control box in the center of the web. They both stared at it in silence. The dark-colored material was so well camouflaged it was a wonder they had seen it at all. The box itself was about half the size of the stealth ship. Every now and then, a spark would send a bright bolt of electric blue along one quadrant, lighting the web-like connectors.

This was by far the most impressive installation of Xakul technology he had ever seen. It had to be destroyed.

"Is there a way to disable it?" He mused, his hands on the controls drifting the shuttle this way and that slowly, trying to see the box from all angles. "Can you think of anything?"

Krystal shook her head slowly. "I've never seen anything like it. If I studied it to see how it works, sure. Then I could work something out. But I have no idea this thing works."

They spent the next few minutes drifting around the

entire network on the jammer. It turned out to be a 3D installation, spreading out over a vast area. The little stealth ship could duck and weave between the connections with ease, T'arq and Krystal collecting as much information about it as possible.

But even with all the scans the stealth ship could run, they couldn't disable it.

Well, there was only one thing to do then.

"We have to get rid of it," he said, shifting his hands on the controls to move their ship away from the signal jammer. When he was satisfied at the distance, he aimed for the central control box and loosed a plasma bomb. The sticky projectile latched onto its target, wrapping dark tendrils around the box.

Krystal gasped. "T'arq! What are you doing?"

He didn't look at her as his hands moved on the controls. "We can't just leave it here like this. It needs to be destroyed."

"But—"

He cut her off. "It's the only thing that makes sense, Krystal." He pointed at the control box, the plasms bomb's tendrils now entirely obscuring it from view. "It's the safest way to destroy it. We'll move well away, detonate the plasma bomb remotely."

"It just seems a little reckless," she huffed, crossing her arms. "They're bound to come and investigate."

T'arq knew she was right, but he had no choice. He moved the ship away to a safe distance and then a little further. He didn't like the idea of taking risks with Krystal's life. His own? Well, he had been a warrior for so long. What was one more risk to his life? But he wouldn't risk hers.

Reckless? That was the last thing he was.

"Detonation in three... two... one." With a simple swipe on the screen, the plasma bomb detonated, spreading debris flying away from where the signal jammer had been. A brief flash was all that signified an explosion had occurred, there not being enough oxygen to fuel a fire for any considerable length of time.

"That was underwhelming."

T'arq laughed, rubbing a hand over his face, and shared a smile with Krystal. He knew she was an incredibly intelligent and capable woman. That wasn't in question. But he also knew that fear could take hold of your thoughts and crowd your head until there was nothing left. He couldn't let that happen to Krystal. Not again.

"Should we try the Zataras?"

"Yes, although—"

A loud wailing filled the cockpit. The alarm quickly shut off by T'arq, who swore under his breath.

"What was that?" The terror in Krystal's voice was palpable.

T'arq's lips pressed into a thin line.

"Can you check the cloak?"

Krystal's breathing was rapid as she rushed to complete the task. Her fingers shaking so badly that T'arq reached across to give her shoulder a reassuring squeeze.

"Um... it's fine. But what was that noise?"

T'arq swallowed. He knew she wouldn't like this, but there was no way around it. She'd find out soon enough whether or not he told her.

"The Xakul are approaching."

This was exactly what he had hoped wouldn't happen.

T'arq had promised Krystal he would keep her safe, that this was a routine mission. How could she trust him now? He had to get her back to the Zataras as soon as possible. But first he had to check in with the Zataras. The crew on the starship had no idea where they were or what they were up against. If anything happened... he swallowed, trying to avoid thinking about that.

He began moving the ship back into the asteroid field, aiming toward a rock barely larger than the stealth ship itself. He opened the comm, hoping that the destruction of the jammer meant they could speak with the starship once more. "Zataras, this is Qu'Ress Alpha."

"Good to hear your voice, Qu'Ress. We lost you for a while there."

"We have identified and destroyed a signal jammer." T'arq rattled off the coordinates. "There are incoming Xakul fighters."

"Received," Tomas' voice filled the comm. "Qu'Ress, I need you to do a sweep of the area before you return. What's your status?"

Krystal shot a horrified look at T'arq, who muted the microphone.

"We need to go." Krystal grabbed at his sleeve. "T'arq! We have to get back to the Zataras. Now!"

T'arq was torn. He agreed with Krystal, but this was such an excellent opportunity to collect valuable intelligence. Too good to pass up. He hated making her even more uncomfortable, and he wondered whether she would ever forgive him for this.

"I'm sorry, Krystal. You heard the captain. We can't leave until I know more."

Krystal banged her head against the headrest on her chair and let out a frustrated squeal.

T'arq opened the channel again. "Systems functioning within normal range. The cloak is working better than I expected."

"Good. Find out what you can. Zataras out."

T'arq closed the comm signal. "We're going to wait for the Xakul, and follow them back to wherever their base is. There will be one nearby." T'arq settled the ship next to the rock and activated the tether to hold it in the rock's gravitational field. He turned to look at her. "We'll be safe here."

He set the scanners to alert him when the Xakul were in visual range. He figured they could hide next to this rock and see what happens. With the cloak hiding them away, they'd be safe here.

"How can you say we'll be safe with the Xakul arriving any second?" The words escaped in a rush as she wrung her hands together.

He placed a hand on her shoulder, his fingers gently easing the tension in her muscles. "The cloak will keep us hidden, won't it?" He waited for her nod before he continued. "It shouldn't take too long for them to arrive. They will want to know what disrupted their signal jammer. I need to know how many Xakul there are. They are far too close to the Zataras for my comfort."

He ran a hand through his hair and stared out the window. "I don't like it either. Everything is screaming at me to take you back right now, but what if they know the Zataras' location? It may not be safe there either."

Krystal nodded reluctantly. "OK."

T'arq released a breath on a long exhalation. "And I need you, Krystal."

Her hands stilled in her lap and she twisted her head him, releasing an indelicate snort.

"You don't believe me?" He lifted an eyebrow. "Taureans operate stealth ships as a pair: the pilot and the flight engineer. I've been managing without a flight engineer, but it's not ideal."

"Why?" She tapped a finger on the armrest of her chair, the same wary expression on her face. Tap, tap.

"I have a reputation—"

"I know all about your reputation." Tap, tap, tap.

T'arq scowled. "That's not what I meant."

"Oh?" Her finger stilled. "What did you mean, then?"

"People think I'm hard to work with."

Krystal's eyebrows raised in surprise. "Really?"

T'arq felt himself flush. Taureans did not blush. But T'arq wasn't entirely Taurean, something he took great pains to hide. He hoped she wouldn't notice. What would she think if she knew what he was?

"Are you blushing?"

"No." He turned away.

The alarm rang out in the cabin. T'arq had never thought he would be relieved to see the Xakul, but here he was.

Krystal shrank back in her seat, reaching for T'arq's hand. He squeezed gently as they watched first one, then two, then what seemed like an entire fleet of fighters stream toward the destroyed signal jammer.

"Holy shit. There's so many," Krystal breathed.

T'arq pressed his lips into a grim line. This was far more

than he had ever seen together. And they would not have sent all their fighters, so this must be a tiny portion of their force.

Why were they here? What did they want?

For long minutes T'arq and Krystal sat in silence watching as the Xakul appeared to inspect the jammer. When the Xakul finally moved away, T'arq realized they had been sitting there holding hands the entire time.

He extracted his hand from Krystal's and moved to power the ship back up.

"Wait!" Krystal's whispered warning had him pausing. "The change in energy might cause the cloak to ripple. I haven't tested that yet."

T'arq nodded, thankful that she had been thinking quickly enough to prevent what could have been a disaster. If the Xakul spotted them, they were as good as dead.

The last ship moved past them, all heading back in the direction they had come. When it was out of sight on the other side of the asteroid, T'arq sent a questioning look at Krystal, who nodded.

He started the engine and moved the ship out from hiding.

They followed the Xakul at a safe distance.

"If only warp trail was a thing," Krystal mumbled at one stage, rubbing her arms with her hands.

"Hmm?"

"Never mind. Can we follow them from further away?"

"No, this is the safest distance. If we drop back any further, we'll lose them."

They were soon flying deeper into the asteroid field, dodging spinning rocks twice the size of their shuttle. T'arq was silent in his focus, keeping their little ship on track.

"Is that where they're going?" Krystal pointed at the biggest asteroid yet, easily twice the size of the Zataras itself, where the ships appeared to be heading. She used the view screen to zoom in. If they continued at that speed, they would smash into the asteroid. What were they doing?

"That's no asteroid," T'arq could not believe what he was seeing. A massive door opened in what appeared to be an asteroid, and the fighters disappeared as if they were specs of dust.

Krystal looked like she was going to be sick.

"How far from Earth are we?"

"Not far enough for my liking with that... base... or whatever it is." T'arq's voice was grim.

He tried to open the comm again, but the same empty channel appeared. "They're using another signal jammer. They must have them everywhere!"

He had to find somewhere for them to hide. "Krystal?"

"Yes?" Her voice was small, her hands gripping the chair arms again, but she didn't sound as afraid as she had been.

"Can you scan for a place for us to hide? Look for a rock with a depression that will fit our ship, and that isn't spinning away from that." He waved his hand at the camouflaged Xakul base.

He could do it himself in seconds, but he thought that giving her something to do might help with her nerves.

"You're trying to get me to focus on something else, aren't you?" she asked as she tapped away on the screen.

He smiled. "Of course not."

"Hmm," was his reply, but he could hear the smile in her voice.

"All right, over here," she gestured to a spot on the screen, zooming in so T'arq could see a shadowed nook just large enough to fit their ship.

T'arq nodded. It was a suitable spot, easily able to view the comings and goings of the Xakul, but hidden within shadows. T'arq slid the ship smoothly into place, but this time he kept the engines idling, not wanting to risk their cloak. The Xakul would scan the area, of that he was absolutely certain. It was impressive how effective Krystal's cloak was, but he was still nervous.

He had to get the information he needed and then get Krystal safely back to the Zataras. He glanced across at her. Her head was down, watching streams of data on her tablet.

"Still running your tests?"

She looked up and grinned. "It's working much better than I had hoped. Even sitting here in partial shadow, it's keeping us hidden."

The AI's voice came over the speakers in the cockpit. "Proximity alert. Incoming object."

T'arq flicked the screen to show the external view of the ship, showing a small, dark object creeping toward them. It was shaped like a disc, flatter than it was wide, and it hovered slowly, though no method of propulsion was visible.

"What is that?" she asked, transfixed by the sinister presence of the dark object. She pushed back in her chair as if she could move further away.

T'arq's voice was grim. "A Xakul drone."

"Do they know we're here?" She watched as the drone drifted closer, the matte black of the exterior making it fade into the darkness of space beyond. If she wasn't staring right at it, it would be easy to miss.

"I'm not sure. It could just be a coincidence..."

"But you don't believe in coincidences, do you?" Krystal's voice was barely above a whisper, as if speaking quietly would prevent the drone from seeing them.

A line of horizontal lights flickered into life, the brightness making T'arq blink and Krystal throw an arm up to shield her eyes.

"No." T'arq watched the drone move closer, the light of what must be a scanner sliding backwards and forward across the asteroid until it was almost on top of them. T'arq's heartbeat was so loud he could hear it in his ears.

"What do we do?" Her words were so quiet, he almost missed them.

"We wait. Hopefully, it will pass over us."

The drone reached them and hovered over the ship. T'arq and Krystal stared, transfixed, as it hovered mere meters away from them, visible through the glass of the cockpit window. The light of the scanner danced over their ship, flickering in the darkened interior. The drone stopped right in front of them as a small hatch on the underside opened and a mechanical arm emerged.

She darted a nervous glance at T'arq. "What is—"

Without warning, the drone fired a small blob of a neon green substance at them, which spread across the glass of the hatch in a web-like pattern.

T'arq had a suspicion he knew exactly what the substance was. "Fuck."

CHAPTER TEN

Krystal

What had just happened? The drone had just flung something... sticky at them?

Glancing at the usually unflappable Taurean next to her, Krystal realized that something was very wrong. His usually golden skin was pale, and his purple eyes were dark with focus. His hands flew over the controls with seemingly unerring accuracy.

Krystal looked from T'arq to the drone, which had retracted the arm and was now hovering in front of them. It hadn't moved since it had stopped.

"What is that stuff?"

"I don't know, not exactly. But they use it as a marker."

T'arq's hands flew faster than Krystal had seen yet, blasting the drone out of existence with the small plasma gun mounted to the exterior of the shuttle.

"T'arq?"

Hands still moving rapidly, he moved the ship out of hiding and, with seemingly no regard for caution, away from the giant Xakul ship and deeper into the asteroid belt. "They know we're here." His voice was grim as he focused. "And they're following."

Krystal paled, hands gripping the armrests tightly. "How? The cloak was working..."

"I don't know. But they knew, and they marked us." His words were clipped, hands manipulating the ship this way and that to deter their pursuers.

As if on cue, the AI's voice filled their headsets. "Proximity alert. Incoming vessels."

"Computer, how many ships?" T'arq barked.

Krystal fought to hold back a wail as the computer replied.

"Seventeen Xakul fighters."

"Fuck." T'arq punched a button on the controls near his head and the little ship shot forward.

"So many?" Krystal gripped the armrests of her seat and squeezed her eyes shut as the ship jerked rapidly from side to side to avoid obstacles.

"Krystal? I need you to use the guns."

Still squeezing her eyes shut, she shook her head. "I can't!"

The ship rolled in a maneuver that had the contents of her stomach threatening to make itself known. She swallowed a groan, hands still squeezing her chair so tightly that she was sure her fingers would have no feeling.

"You must." T'arq's voice was calm, belying the frantic movements of his hands as the ship bobbed and weaved to escape the Xakul tailing them.

Krystal took a breath, fighting panic as she willed her heart to calm.

"Trust me?" he asked.

Surprise had her eyes flying open as the response came immediately. "With my life."

He nodded and gestured at the screen in front of her. "There are controls for the rear guns here. One is a plasma cannon. Only use that if you are certain that you have a perfect shot. This ship wasn't designed for sustained combat, so there isn't much ammunition."

She nodded, memorizing the control where he had gestured.

"The other is a laser gun."

"A what?" She had never heard of a laser gun, which meant that—

"It's new technology," T'arq said, a note of something she couldn't quite identify in his voice.

Focusing back on the laser gun, she pulled up the rear view of the ship. They were dodging and weaving amongst asteroids, some of them the size of a house, others merely football-sized. She knew it made no difference. Even a small piece of space debris could cause significant damage if it struck them.

Krystal swallowed past the lump that had formed in her throat and pushed the thought aside. There was a job to do, and she would do it. Touching the controls, she moved the guns around to get used to them and then sighted on the first Xakul ship.

"Not yet," T'arq cautioned. "They're not in range. Wait until the sight on the gun turns green and then hit the automatic targeting."

She nodded, eyes narrowing as she watched the Xakul ship approach and gain on them. T'arq whipped the ship around a rock the size of a bus, and the enemy disappeared.

Focusing on her breathing, Krystal kept her finger ready on the trigger. The Xakul ship rounded the rock, and she fired. The first blast with the laser gun missed, and she realized she had forced the gun off target. She tried again, this time trusting the automatic targeting. The laser cut into the ship, and it spun into the asteroid, breaking into scattered debris.

She gaped. She, a civilian who struggled to kill a cockroach, had just taken out a Xakul ship.

"Nice work!" T'arq's voice broke through her stunned silence.

"Only sixteen more to go," she muttered. How could they possibly survive this?

Krystal had no time to think, as one after another the Xakul ships bored down on them.

"Why aren't they firing at us?" Krystal asked as she shot down the third fighter.

T'arq was silent for a long moment as he rolled the ship up and over a piece of space junk that looked like it had once been a ship. Krystal's eyes fixed on the wreckage; the hull torn apart. Snaked cabling floated from the wreck, like seaweed in the ocean. Light glinted from the glassy panels of what must have once been the bridge. As they shot past, Krystal glimpsed bodies strapped to chairs inside the wreck.

T'arq's voice jerked her back to the present. "I suspect they want to capture us."

"What?" the thought horrified Krystal. She knew what the Xakul did to people. Laila had seen it and, before Krystal had come to Taurean space, she had warned her what contact with the evil insectoid aliens would become. "No fucking way! Not if I have anything to say about it!"

Krystal turned with renewed focus to the Xakul fighters, who were getting too close for comfort. Time passed in a blur. What could have been minutes could also have been hours, Krystal again and again taking down Xakul ships.

When there was half the original number left, T'arq let out a startled intelligible shout, before jerking the ship downwards in a sudden move that had Krystal feeling light-headed. Before she knew what was happening, the ship jolted, and they were rolling and rolling, end of end, before stopping with a bone-rattling bang. Krystal was thrown around in her seat, but thanks to T'arq ensuring she was strapped in tightly, she did not slip out.

The interior lights of the ship flickered and went out, the AI's voice distorted before being cut off. Krystal blinked to clear her vision, her head pounding. A bright light speared into the cockpit, and she lifted a hand to shield her eyes. As her vision cleared, she saw the looming hulk of one of the Xakul ships closing in on them.

As they came closer, Krystal stared in horror as a claw extended and attached to their stealth ship with a jolt that shook her in her seat. They had to get out of here.

She shot a look at T'arq, whose head was lolling to one side, his eyes shut.

Krystal reached across to grab his shoulder, jerking as the straps held her in her seat. She reached to undo the clip and slid out of her harness. The artificial gravity on the ship was, thankfully, still functioning, and she quickly made her way to T'arq.

"T'arq? Wake up." She squeezed his shoulder and gave him a small shake to get his attention, hoping that he wasn't injured, and she wasn't hurting him further.

He groaned and rolled his head away from her.

Encouraged, she shook him again. "T'arq? Come on. We need to get out of here."

His eyes opened slightly and then slammed shut. The light! She put herself in front of him to block the lights from the Xakul. He opened his eyes slightly again, then closed them with a sigh.

"T'arq? The Xakul are here. I need you!" Her words were rushed, and she threw caution to the wind and gave him a hard shake. If he was injured and she made it worse, then it couldn't be worse than the Xakul capturing them.

"What?" He shot upright, arrested by the seat's straps.

Krystal blew out a breath in relief. "The Xakul are here. There's some kind of hook thing, and I don't know what to do!"

T'arq undid his straps and lifted Krystal bodily to move her out of the way.

The second hook latched onto their ship and jerked it away from the asteroid where they had come to a rest. Krystal and T'arq both stumbled and landed against the wall, a cabinet opening with the impact and spraying its contents into the cockpit.

T'arq grasped Krystal by the shoulders and looked at her intently, his eyes deep purple in their intensity. "Are you hurt?"

"What? No. I'm fine. I bumped my head a little, but the helmet... I'm fine."

"Good." He appeared to relax a little at her words. "I've not heard of them doing this before."

Krystal started at T'arq, horrified. That could mean only one of two things: either the Xakul were trying something new, or anyone who had been captured like this had not survived to tell the tale.

Either option was not appealing.

"We have to get out of here." The ship was dead in the water, but surely they could get it going again. Getting rid of the claw things would be a trickier task.

T'arq nodded. "We have to abandon the ship."

He hadn't just said what she thought he had said? He didn't mean that they were to go out into space. Without the protection of even this little ship. She laughed nervously. "That headache must be worse than I thought. I could have sworn you said to abandon the ship."

T'arq's gaze held hers, his purple eyes steady and unblinking.

"No. Nope. Not going to happen." She stepped back from him, punctuating her words with a swipe of her hand.

"We don't have a choice, Krystal." He rubbed his hand over his face. "Look. That stuff they blasted onto us? It's tracking nano-bots. We can't get rid of them. There's an emergency stasis pod that we can use. It's designed to transport dangerous prisoners, but you can use it."

"What?" That sounded like a horrible idea. Being put to sleep with no idea if or where she would wake up. "No."

"All right, then the other option is to suit up and hope that we get picked up before our oxygen runs out."

Krystal's legs gave out from under her, T'arq catching her in his arms before she hit the floor.

Big breaths. In and out. It's going to be ok.

The repeated words ran through her head like a mantra. Closing her eyes, she clutched at the soft, but strong, fabric of T'arq's flight suit with her fingers. His sheer mass was comforting. Surely nothing bad could happen when he was here to protect her?

Breathe. In and out.

The ship jerked again, and Krystal let out an involuntary scream.

"What's it to be Krystal? Do we stay and get captured by the Xakul? Or do we get off this ship?"

CHAPTER ELEVEN

T'arq

He hated making her choose, but from what he knew of Krystal, she had to at least have some control over the situation. He was pleased when she let go of his flight suit, took a deep breath, and nodded at him decisively.

"Let's get out of here."

He smiled in relief. T'arq had no desire to be picked up by the Xakul, nothing good would come of that. He would much rather risk the cold of space than come face to face with those insect bastards.

"Let's get suited up then." T'arq handed Krystal a package wrapped in a silver-colored slinky material. He undid the closure that held the bag shut, gesturing for Krystal to do the same. He held out the matte silver-colored suit, a large ring around the neck the only rigid part. "Step into the suit like this," he said, demonstrating, "and then stretch the suit so the ring goes over your head." T'arq did so, stretching the fabric like an elastic band.

Despite the seriousness of the situation, his lips twitched as he watched Krystal struggle with the suit. He should have expected that a suit designed for a seven-foot-tall Taurean warrior would not fit a much smaller human. The suit sagged around her, making her look as if she had been playing dress-ups.

"You're laughing at me? Really?" She gave up the fight with the silver fabric and put her hands on her hips. It would have looked much more menacing if she didn't look like she had been swallowed by a parachute.

He schooled his features back under control. "No, of course not."

"Hmm." She crossed her arms in front of her chest.

"Are you ready?" He reached to hold the sleeves for her so she could put one arm, then the other, into the suit.

"For what?" she grumbled, reluctantly donning the rest of the suit.

T'arq checked nothing was caught in the closure that ran from hip to opposite shoulder, and flicked a button at the inside neck of the suit.

"Oh!" Krystal exclaimed as the suit adjusted to her smaller size, but not restrictively so. She moved around to look down at herself, then turned to T'arq with raised eyebrows. "This is amazing!"

He grinned, then checked the fit of her suit before adjusting his own. "We'll use these helmets outside." He opened a hatch as he spoke and retrieved two matching helmets. "And we will wear these," he pulled out two backpacks fitted with oxygen tanks.

Just as he passed one backpack to Krystal, the ship jolted again, a reminder that they were running out of time.

"Shit." She scrambled to catch the backpack as it slipped from her hands.

He caught the strap and handed it to her. "It's OK. I'll get you out of here." He hoped he sounded more confident than he felt. T'arq had been in stickier situations, of course, but this time it felt like the consequences were much more dire. He could let nothing happen to Krystal. He would do whatever he could to keep her safe.

He helped Krystal put on the backpack and adjust the straps to fit, securing the oxygen to her helmet. "Krystal?"

She stopped fiddling with one of the backpack straps and looked up at him, brown eyes wide in her pale face. "Yes?"

"It's going to be OK. Trust me?"

She nodded, then stood on her toes to press a quick kiss to his lips. It was so fleeting that he thought he had imagined it, but the flush of color across her cheeks told him he hadn't.

"Why...?"

"If anything happens to me, let Laila know that I—"

"Nothing is going to happen to you!" He growled.

She raised an eyebrow and braced a hand against the wall in the small cargo area as another jerk from the Xakul's claw tossed them into each other. "That's hard to believe."

The lights flickered again, and an ominous groaning noise sounded from the hull over their heads.

She held still, looking upwards as T'arq lifted her helmet and placed it over her head. A click and rotation and the bubble-like helmet slid into place.

T'arq pressed a button on her sleeve. "This is the comm. It's built into the suit. The oxygen will last twelve hours—"

"Only twelve hours?"

"As long as you don't exert yourself. It will last less time if you hyperventilate, so it's incredibly important that you keep as calm as possible."

T'arq smiled sadly as he heard Krystal hum a jerky tune through the comm.

Quickly donning his own backpack, he hooked up the oxygen tank to the helmet and put it on, securing it. He thumbed his comm and held out his elbow. "Shall we?"

"Sure, why not?" Krystal replied with a nervous laugh.

He smiled in what he hoped was a reassuring way. "Disengaging the artificial gravity and opening the hatch. Ready?" When Krystal nodded, he grabbed her around the waist and hooked his arm through one of the tie-down loops used to secure cargo. "Computer, disengage artificial gravity."

"Disengaging artificial gravity."

With a silent prayer that the strap would hold, T'arq kicked the hatch lever open. A rush of air whipped past them as the ship de-pressurized. T'arq grunted as Krystal jerked in his arms, his shoulder complaining as he took the force. Their feet left the floor, pulled closer to the hatch. Thankfully, the ship being small meant it was only a few seconds before it was over.

"Would they have seen?" Krystal asked in a hushed voice.

"Probably, but we'll have to risk it."

"What about my data?" Krystal turned and pulled herself into the cockpit.

T'arq followed to see her retrieve her tablet from where it was floating above her seat, miraculously unbroken.

"Weren't there something like ten of those ships before?" Krystal said, leaning over the seat to look at the tablet that was still showing a scan of the exterior of the ship. It must run on backup power.

T'arq held out his hand and Krystal passed him the tablet. He flicked through the screens to check the exterior, smiling in triumph as he realized the rest of the Xakul had left it to the one ship to bring them in.

One ship he could deal with.

"Change of plans."

T'arq held the charge in one hand, his laser pistol in the other. It wasn't the best thought-out plan, but he didn't have time to come up with anything else. So it would just have to do. The most important thing was getting Krystal to safety and that he could manage.

"So, let's go over the plan again," he said, turning to face her and taking her shoulders in his hands so she wouldn't spin away. He hooked one foot under his pilot's seat and the other was braced against the floor, keeping them still. For once, Krystal's head was at the same level as his, her feet floating above the floor.

"We will be tethered so we don't lose each other," Krystal said, her voice sounding like it was coming from a long distance away because of static from the speakers in his helmet.

"You will go first, aiming for the nearest asteroid that looks large enough to hide us." He nodded in the direction of the Xakul ship. "I will get the plasma cannon, and fire it at the Xakul."

Krystal nodded. "And use the force of the blast to propel yourself away from here and clear of the blast." Krystal's brows furrowed. "That seems a little..."

"Stupid? Probably." He rubbed her shoulders, even though he knew she would probably not feel it through the fabric. "I don't have a better idea." He shrugged. "That's why you have to be well clear when I fire the cannon. If we're too close..." He shook his head.

Krystal jerked under his hands. "Oh! I have an idea." She twisted from his grip and pulled herself about the cabin. T'arq watched as she ripped open anything she could get her hands on, pulling electronic parts out of the ship until, a short while later, she held a small collection in her hands. "I think I might have the answer," she said, excitement making her words quick as she focused. T'arq smiled when she turned to him and held a device the size of her palm out for his inspection. "Tah-dah!" She cried triumphantly, an excited smile splitting her face.

"What is it?" he asked, taking it from her to turn over in his hand.

"A timer."

They shared a grin. Perfect.

Or perfectly stupid. This was probably the stupidest idea he had ever had, but it was this or deal with the Xakul and once they got the ship to their base, there was no knowing what they would do to them. Nobody came back from being captured by the Xakul.

No. This was the only option. They would set a charge on a timer and both escape together. That would be the safest option.

T'arq steadied himself to jump out of the open hatch and glanced at Krystal. "Ready?"

She nodded. "Ready as I'll ever be."

"Do you have the tablet with your data?"

Krystal patted the pocket on the side of her backpack. "Right here."

"Good. Let's go."

Before T'arq could step out, another bang sounded on the hull, and a shadow loomed on the outside of the hatch. One dark claw curled its way through the open hatch, then another until there were six.

T'arq pushed Krystal behind him and drew the pistol from the holster on his thigh. He aimed it through the open hatch and, as the head of the Xakul soldier appeared, he fired.

The Xakul screamed in rage and pulled itself into the cargo hold, the sheer mass of the insect-like alien taking up most of the space. Two of its legs reached for T'arq, who pulled a knife from a sheath at his ankle and sliced in warning through the air.

"Go! Get out of here! Use the cockpit hatch!" T'arq yelled.

"But—"

"If you stay, we're both dead! Go!" T'arq grunted as he threw up an arm to block a blow. He didn't turn to see Krystal go, but he heard her swear softly as she pushed through the cockpit hatch.

"T'arq?"

"Go!"

Fighting a Xakul in close quarters was never a good idea. Their exoskeleton acted like natural armor, making it extremely difficult to land a killing blow. A plasma pistol could do some damage if used at exactly the right location, but the best bet was to blast it with a plasma cannon. But with Krystal on the ship and in such close quarters, T'arq knew that a blast from a plasma cannon would kill them both.

"I'm out." Krystal's voice hitched over the comm.

T'arq dodge and weaved, avoiding the four arms of the Xakul as it used its lower legs to brace against the sides of the small hold. "Are you out of range?"

"Why? What are you going to do?"

He spun through the air, the lack of gravity working for him as he moved behind the Xakul soldier.

"Plasma cannon."

"No! T'arq, you'll kill yourself."

"Are you out of range?" He spun in the air, wrapping a tangling cable around the neck of the Xakul and pulling tight, his feet on its back as he strained. Muscles straining, he grunted as he pulled with all his might.

"Yes," came the whispered reply.

T'arq's arms straining, he found extra strength and with a final jerk; the Xakul went limp.

He pulled himself out of the hatch on the underside of the ship, holding onto the handholds usually used for climbing to the cockpit. He looked over the side of the ship. The Xakul fighter was still there, the hooks attached to the ship dragging it along in little bumpy jerks. As he watched, Xakul soldiers emerged from a hatch and swarmed down toward the stealth ship.

More of the bastards.

Grabbing the plasma cannon he had slung over his shoulder, he aimed for the center of the group of Xakul and fired.

CHAPTER TWELVE

Krystal

With one hand gripping the edge of the cockpit hatch, Krystal glanced up at the Xakul ship hovering ominously above her. The two ships were tethered together in three places, one at the nose of the small stealth ship and two at the rear.

She had only stepped outside of the vessel with T'arq's encouragement, and the thought of what exactly that Xakul soldier would do to her if she didn't make it to safety. She swallowed past the lump that had formed in her throat. It didn't bear thinking about, or she'd freeze and never get away from here.

"T'arq?" It just felt wrong to go without him, like she was missing a limb. Her chest squeezed at the thought.

"Go!" his reply was muffled by a grunt of exertion.

She hesitated, one hand on the ship holding tight to the edge of the hatch while she stared at the great expanse of space spread in front of her. While the Xakul ship had been towing them, they had left the depths of the asteroid belt. She had never been skydiving. The thought had terrified her, but this felt so much worse. At least there weren't so many obstacles to crash into here. It looked like this was it. She either went now or she faced the Xakul. Her stomach clenched, and she fought nausea. Vomiting in your space suit would not be a good way to start her first spacewalk. She took a deep breath, closed her eyes, and pushed off with her legs as hard as she could.

"I'm out," she whispered, not wanting to open her eyes.

It had taken all of Krystal's courage to push off from the ship and send herself drifting into the deep cold of space. Thousands of years of evolution were screaming inside her that this was a terrible idea, but she trusted T'arq. With her life, she realized.

With every second, she drifted further and further away from the ship, and further and further away from T'arq.

Oh god. I should have stayed!

She panicked, eyes flying open as she rolled onto her back to watch the ship as she drifted away. Her heart pounded in her chest as she fought to keep her breathing calm. To conserve oxygen, she had to stay calm. She counted backwards from ten slowly, trying to calm her rapid breathing and her frantically beating heart.

"Are you out of range?" T'arq's deep voice filled her helmet, and she squeezed her eyes shut.

"Why? What are you going to do?" Please don't let him be doing anything stupid. All he had to do was set the timer and come out after her. He still had time... didn't he?

The reply did not reassure her. "Plasma cannon."

What? A plasma cannon in such close quarters would rip

the ship to shreds... and everything inside it. It was suicide! "No! T'arq, you'll kill yourself."

"Are you out of range?"

"Yes," she whispered. Eyes wide in horror, she watched as dark shapes swarmed down the tethers from the Xakul vessel to enter the stealth ship.

She hit the comm, "T'arq—"

A flash of light had her lifting her head to see the ship engulfed in a fireball that winked out almost as fast as it had begun. She gasped.

Oh no.

Krystal sobbed into her helmet. Unable to wipe her tears, they ran unchecked down her face. What had he done? Why hadn't she stayed? She might have been able to help.

She blinked to clear her vision, horrified at what she saw. Where the stealth ship had been was a single panel that dangled from one of the broken tethers. The Xakul ship spun in a lazy circle, the two remaining tethers flailing and unattached.

T'arq!

She blinked, fighting to clear her tears. He was gone. There was no way he could have survived that blast if he even made it that long. How many Xakul had there been? She had been too stunned to count. Too many for him to fight on his own. She felt sick.

But what about the Xakul base they had discovered? She had to get the information back to the Zataras. They were so close to Earth's solar system that it could only be an advanced launching pad for an attack on Earth.

Krystal forced herself to slow her breathing. "I can do this." She chanted the words until her voice became firm.

And T'arq? He would want her to stay calm. If she was to get out of this, she had to stay calm.

She straightened, and taking a deep breath, turned on her back to survey her surroundings. When Krystal had pushed off from the ship, she had aimed for the biggest of the asteroids she could see, hoping for a place to hide in until she could be rescued.

She had got quite close to it and, turning onto her back, realized that if she released a little of the oxygen from the tank on her back, she could propel herself close enough to climb onto it.

But how much oxygen did she have?

According to the display on her comm, the tank was close to full. There was nothing for it but to try.

Krystal lined herself up with the asteroid and, locating the oxygen vent on the backpack, released a quick burst, barely even a second. She moved closer to the asteroid, but achingly slowly. She harrumphed.

"Once more and we'll get to you, you big bastard," she spoke as if the asteroid was listening to her.

She released another burst of oxygen, this time enough that she could grasp the edge of the rocky surface and hold on.

"Oof!" The air rushed out of her lungs at the impact as her body swung and hit the rock. "Ouch." Her knee ached where she had struck it, but the suit seemed to be no worse for wear. Thankfully.

She had landed near a small depression in the rock, big enough to shield her, but only barely. It would have to do.

Krystal tucked herself into the small space, bracing her back against one side and her feet against the other. The asteroid had a little gravity, but not so much that she wouldn't drift away if she wasn't careful. It made no difference, she knew, but being next to the bulk of the large rock reassured her a little.

From where she sat, she could see the Xakul ship and the wreckage of the stealth ship. Her breath hitched.

Don't think about him. Plenty of time for that later. Hopefully.

She checked her oxygen levels. There were a little over eight hours before things became dire. Krystal fumbled at her wrist for the comm, cycling through the screens until she reached the emergency beacon. She hit the button for the emergency locator, her breath releasing with a rush of relief. Now to just sit and wait. And hope.

Eight hours to think.

Wrapping her arms around her legs, she rested her head on her knees and stared at the wreckage of the ship. It felt like her heart had torn into as many pieces as the ship. She buried her head into her arms and sobbed.

———

A buzzing noise woke her from a doze. Frantically, she checked the time. Only an hour had passed. Her eyes were sore, her lashes clumped together. Had it only been that morning that she had been arguing with T'arq? And now he was dead. Her eyes filled with tears again.

The buzzing noise came again, Krystal dragged her tablet out of the side pocket of her backpack. Something was broadcasting on the frequency that the Taurean military used. Was someone nearby?

She blinked rapidly to clear her vision and looked up at

where the Xakul ship had been, alarmed to see that it was now much closer than it had been before.

Why hadn't they left?

Krystal belatedly recalled the magnification function in the tablet and, pointing it at the Xakul ship, enlarged the view.

Something dull and silver was attached to the exterior of the Xakul ship. She enlarged the view again; the image becoming grainy and difficult to focus.

It wasn't a thing; it was a person. It didn't matter what the chances were, she had to get to him.

Had he survived?

Before she knew what she was doing, she had stashed her tablet and pulled the backpack on. She couldn't live with herself if there was even a slight chance he was alive, and she didn't do everything she could to help him.

She braced her feet against the rock and with all the force she could muster, flung herself off the asteroid and toward the Xakul ship.

Not fast enough!

She swore, fumbling with her oxygen tank to release the precious gas to propel herself closer. Her heart raced as she approached.

Please, please let it be him.

A gasp escaped her as she drew closer, the seconds seeming to crawl as she closed the distance.

"T'arq!"

There was no reply. His helmet might be damaged, or he might be unconscious. She felt a renewed purpose. She had to get to him.

She flew at the ship. Shit. She was going too fast. She had

to slow down. Krystal fumbled with the oxygen, aiming the hose toward the Xakul ship, but it barely slowed her speed.

If she hit the ship, it would be like hitting concrete, and if she missed... well, she would just continue on. The chances of her being picked up were slim to none, if that happened. She had so little oxygen left that she might as well just give up now if she missed.

One chance. She had one chance to get this right.

She expelled as much from the tank as she dared, secured the line so she had both hands free and pulled the loose belt strap from her waist. The ship was approaching fast now, and she frantically tied a loop in the end of the belt and held it in one hand as she spread her arms and legs as wide as possible.

All she needed was to grab onto something and hold on. She would deal with whatever damaged she did to herself afterwards. But if she missed, then it was over anyway.

The ship loomed large as she approached, rushing to meet her.

Krystal hit the side of the ship dead on, her hands flailing to catch a hold on the surface.

"Fuck!" She rolled along it, spinning and missed her hand holds. Her breath escaped in a rush, her vision swimming as tears flooded her eyes. Where was T'arq?

She spun again and lost track of him. Krystal blinked, forcing herself to focus. What could she grab to hold on to? It felt like time slowed as she tumbled over the ship and rolled underneath it, the asteroid she had been on disappearing rapidly in the distance. Her focus narrowed to the strap held in her hand. She outstretched her arm, hoping to loop the strap over something and halt her movement. Turning her head, she caught sight of the tether flailing near her. She spun, flung the strap out and over a bolt that was sticking out at an odd angle.

She held onto the strap with both hands, closed her eyes and braced for the jolt. Her shoulders felt like someone had jerked them out of their sockets and she screamed in agony, but held on. Everything in her was focused on holding onto that strap. Her fingers slid, jerkily, down the strap until she was barely holding on. Her fingers burned with the exertion as she flailed back in the other direction, kicking her legs wildly to move closer to the tether.

She pulled one hand over the other along the belt toward the metal of the tether, and not a moment too soon. The bolt gave way, and she lunged for the safety of the tether. Gasping for breath, she clung to the metal anchored to the Xakul ship.

That had been the most terrifying things she had ever done. She scrunched her eyes shut until she felt her breathing slow.

T'arq. Where was he?

She turned her head to look up at the Xakul ship. His limp body dangling uselessly. She had to get to him.

The tether flailed back and forth, Krystal hanging from the end. It wasn't safe yet. She needed to get away from all the debris that was floating nearby. Glancing back at the asteroid, she realized just how foolish her actions had been. She could have struck a piece of the destroyed ship and been killed.

But I wasn't.

Krystal pushed the thought aside and, fixing her sights on T'arq's distant still form, she began to pull herself arm over arm, up the tether, moving steadily closer to him.

Was he still alive?

Frantically she scrambled across the underside of the

ship, finding whatever she could use as a handhold, until she reached his side.

"T'arq? Can you hear me?" She held her breath, waiting for a reply.

Please don't be dead. I don't think I could survive without you.

CHAPTER THIRTEEN

T'arq

Voices drifted around him but, no matter how he tried, he couldn't quite grasp their meaning. He felt he should know who was speaking—the voices were familiar—but every time he tried to think of a name; it disappeared like smoke. There were two of them. A soft and calm voice, and one more sharp as if used to giving commands.

The softer voice—a woman—said something, which was followed by a mumbled reply T'arq couldn't quite catch. He drifted in and out of consciousness, their voices muffled.

"... not much left..."

"... surprised he's still breathing..."

The words drifted through his... helmet? Why wasn't he wearing his helmet?

"... big bastard."

"... will she be OK?"

Who were they talking about? Krystal? It had to be Krystal.

"Hopefully."

"... hasn't woken... dangerously low on oxygen..."

Krystal! He had to get to her. T'arq tried to clear his throat to speak, but groaned at the effort and tried to sit up.

"All right, big guy. Settle down." A small hand pushed him back onto the bed. It was almost comical how weak he was.

"Krystal..." he mumbled, before exhaustion overtook him and he dropped back into unconsciousness.

———

Sometime later, he eased his eyes open. Bright light speared his aching head, and he slammed his eyes shut. Shit.

"Sub-Commander Qu'Ress? T'arq? Can you hear me?" That was not Krystal.

"Krystal," he muttered, pushing to sit up and squinting into the bright lights. "Krystal!" He roared, pushing off the bed. *The bed?* That he was on and stumbling across the floor to catch himself with a hand against the wall. "Krystal!" He bellowed again.

"Sub-Commander!" The gasped voice came from behind him, and he spun, blinking, until the fuzzy outline of a woman came into slight focus. Her red hair framed her face like a halo and she cowered in the corner.

Before he could take a step closer, he was grabbed from behind and lifted bodily and thrown back on the bed. He rose on his elbows to glare at Oren.

"She's safe, you idiot." Oren growled at him.

T'arq flopped back down on the bed in relief, turning his head to face his fellow warrior. "I have to see her."

The older Taurean shot him a glare, daring him to move, before turning a much softer gaze to the woman in the corner. "Amelia, come," he bent and picked her up, cradling her in his arms. "Do not scare the doctor who has been caring for your... flight engineer." Oren lifted an eyebrow.

"Flight engineer?" T'arq's brows drew together in confusion.

Oren scoffed, turning and walking to the doorway, where he paused. "Do you want to see her or not?"

T'arq scrambled from the bed and followed, the room swimming before his eyes and using the walls to hold himself up as he moved. Cool air brushed against him, and he realized that his clothing and boots had been removed and he was wearing the single-use garments patients wore when in medical. The corridor was tiny, the familiar layout letting T'arq know he was on a Taurean shuttle used for longer distance freight hauling between systems.

Oren turned into a room, T'arq following to see him put the human doctor back on her feet. She smiled up at him and brushed her hand against his cheek before turning to the slight form lying in the bed.

"Krystal." T'arq practically fell forward in his haste to get to her side, collapsing in the chair next to her bed. She was still in her flight suit, the deep purple color at odds with the white walls and steel of the rest of the room. A medical monitor was hovering over the bed, the large curved white device passing in lazy paths over her body. The accelerated healing it provided gave a pink flush to her skin. She looked like a beautiful, but wilted, flower. Her eyes were closed and

T'arq felt his own chest loosen as he watched hers rise and fall slowly with her breath.

She was alive. After all they had been through, they were both alive.

"How did you...?"

"Find you?" Oren replied, lazing against the wall with his arms crossed.

T'arq nodded.

"I guessed it wasn't you who activated the emergency beacon. You're lucky to be alive. Both of you." Came the gruff reply.

"How did we get here?" T'arq had no recollection of what had happened after he had shot at the Xakul with the plasma cannon, fully expecting to not survive.

"You were unconscious and had hooked your backpack on the underside of the Xakul ship."

"Not on purpose."

Oren chuckled. "I didn't think so, not by the way it had pierced your backup oxygen tank."

T'arq paled.

"Yes, exactly. And she," he nodded at Krystal where she lay in the bed, "had clipped herself into the tether next to you."

Amelia began moving about her patient, checking various equipment and recording readings that were alien to T'arq. He stared at Krystal's peaceful form. In sleep, her face was relaxed, no worry lines between her brows or crinkling at the corner of her eyes when she laughed. She was peaceful. He reached across to take her hand in his, brushing his thumb across the back of her hand.

She mumbled in her sleep, and he smiled.

"She shouldn't have been there."

"No shit."

T'arq shot the older warrior a sharp look. "No, you don't understand. She didn't want to come. I had to work to convince her. She was so scared." His eyes roved over her face. He lent forward to brush his fingers lightly over her forehead, tucking a stray lock of hair behind her ear. "I shouldn't have made her do it." He looked up at Oren. "The cloak? I don't know how she did it, but it works! Or it did until a Xakul drone hit us with some kind of marker." He sat back in his chair, twisting his hands in his lap. "We couldn't escape them, and then they boarded the ship, so I sent her away. On a space walk by herself. It was that or be grabbed by those asshole cockroaches and I couldn't let that happen." He almost growled the last words. "When I knew she was far enough away that she would be safe, I blasted them with the plasma cannon."

Oren chuckled and leaned against the wall; arms crossed against his broad chest. "You crazy bastard."

T'arq's face twisted as he watched Krystal's chest rise and fall with her breath. "Too crazy for her. I almost got her killed." He could barely believe they had both survived. "She deserves so much better," he added quietly.

Amelia finished checking her patient. "T'arq? She was dangerously low on oxygen, the tank almost empty. She was unconscious when we reached you, and I'm not sure for how long."

T'arq's brow knitted. She should have had plenty of oxygen. He'd made sure her tanks were full. He looked away from Krystal to meet the doctor's questioning gaze. "Is she going to recover?"

"I hope so, but we'll know for sure when she wakes up. Are you planning on staying here with her?"

T'arq frowned. Where else would he go? "Of course."

"I'll bring you something to eat."

He nodded his thanks, noticing the way she stood close to Oren and the possessive hand the intelligence operative had placed on her shoulder. "Thank you." T'arq wondered just how much the two had shared. Did she know about the team? They could do with a doctor, with the number of scrapes they got into.

When Amelia had left the room, T'arq turned his gaze to Oren. "So, how much does she know?"

Oren shrugged. "Enough."

T'arq's gaze narrowed. Sometimes the former intelligence operative forgot he wasn't working by himself anymore and made decisions without thinking about the impacts on others on the team.

He wondered how much Krystal knew. She wasn't a member of the human Space Force, but then again, neither was her sister Laila, not anymore. He didn't like keeping secrets, which was part of the reason that he didn't get close to many people. There was only so much you could tell someone before you bordered on divulging critical information.

"There's a problem," T'arq admitted.

Oren leaned against the wall and lifted an eyebrow in question, his thumbs hooked in his pockets. "Apart from the Xakul drone seeing through the cloak?"

T'arq frowned. "We ran into a signal jammer. Bigger than anything I've seen before, and much more effective than the small-scale ones. We destroyed it, which brought Xakul fighters out into the open." He rubbed a hand over his face, his stomach twisting at the thought of just how close he had come to losing Krystal. To them both dying.

"That seems a little foolhardy." Oren sent a significant gaze in Krystal's direction where she lay on the bed.

T'arq scowled, but nodded. "Yes. I wouldn't do it again, but Tomas ordered it." He stared down at the prone form of Krystal, lying so still in the bed. If he could go back... but that wasn't worth thinking about. What was done was done.

"Ah." Oren pushed off from the wall and came to stand next to T'arq.

"They're preparing an assault." T'arq turned his head, purple eyes serious as he met Oren's cool aqua blue gaze.

"On Earth?" One eyebrow lifted in question.

"Where else?"

Oren nodded, rubbing his chin in thought. "There isn't anywhere else they could hit, not from there."

The two Taureans were silent for long moments, considering the consequences of a Xakul attack on Earth. The humans were so ill-equipped to face an enemy like the Xakul the outcome was obvious. And would be as terrible as it would be quick.

"It would be a massacre," T'arq stated boldly.

"A total annihilation," Oren agreed.

"We can't let this happen."

"I concur."

"We have to keep them safe." Not that T'arq had done such a good job of that so far. All he had to do was keep Krystal safe. That was his one job on this test flight. T'arq rubbed a hand over his face and sighed. So much for that. She lay in a medical bay bed, unconscious!

T'arq brushed his fingers over the back of her small hand, then taking it in his own to feel her pulse jerk against his fingers. He sat there, drinking in everything about her; the freckles over her nose, the long brown lashes that curved against her cheeks, the way her hair curled wildly. He committed it all to memory.

She had saved them both, and he had done... what, exactly? He'd flown them into a Xakul fleet, got them caught, shot at, and sent her on a solo spacewalk, the outcome of which was so poor that he may as well have sent her to her death. And she had survived and saved them both.

He knew she was attracted to him, but he also knew that she didn't want something temporary. His track record was just that—temporary. How could he offer her anything more? Why would she want anything more with him?

Enough people had told him of his reputation, and he was beginning to think they had a point. What was that brilliant Earth saying? If it looked like a duck and quacked like a duck?

He was jerked from his thoughts by Krystal, her eyelashes fluttering against her cheeks as she woke. He held his breath. Would she be all right?

Krystal's head rolled around on the pillow, her eyes opening to mere slits, as if the light in the room hurt. "T'arq?" Her voice was croaky, hardly recognizable.

"I'm here," he squeezed her hand.

"I found you." She smiled at him, and he had never been so glad in his life. "I saw you on the ship and I came to you."

"How?"

"I used the oxygen tank."

"To propel yourself?" His eyes widened.

"Yes." She smiled. "It worked."

"You could have died."

"But I didn't."

He sat back in the chair and stared at her. "I didn't deploy the emergency beacon."

"I did it."

He nodded. She had done everything. The little human who had struggled to even get onto the ship in the first place had saved them. And all he'd done was knock himself out with a plasm cannon blast.

He'd promised to keep her safe. Promised her it was just a test flight, and that nothing bad would happen to her.

He'd broken his promise.

"I didn't keep you safe." He pulled his hand out of hers and looked away, unable to meet her eyes.

"T'arq?"

He looked down at his hands. He had promised Zac and Laila he'd keep her safe, that he'd look out for her. But, more importantly, he promised her that nothing would happen to her. That the trip would be routine. And she'd almost died.

She had trusted him and look what had happened!

"I wouldn't be here if it wasn't for you."

T'arq felt his insides twist at her words. Of that, he was absolutely certain. His actions had put her in this hospital bed. He could have found another way to test her cloak. He could have refused to follow the Xakul fighters. He could have pulled away. It was all his fault. Everything was his fault.

Krystal had almost died because of him.

He took a deep breath and squeezed his eyes shut, not wanting to see her face. He couldn't cope if he looked at her and saw accusation in her eyes. "I know," he said, a hitch in his voice, his face pale. He swallowed. "It won't happen again." He fought to get the words out before turning and leaving the room.

"T'arq!" she called out after him.

He paused in the doorway, his back to her, then squared his shoulders, turned and left.

CHAPTER FOURTEEN

Krystal

What had just happened? Krystal stared at the empty doorway that T'arq had filled only moments before. She had been so happy to see him—to see that he was unharmed—and then... what exactly had that been all about?

Krystal ran their conversation through her head, trying to figure out what she had done to send him away. She shook her head.

Amelia appeared in the doorway holding a tray, Oren right behind her. "You're awake, I see." At her bright voice, Krystal gave a small smile.

"T'arq..." she trailed off.

Amelia moved into the room to put the tray on a table beside the bed. She smiled and patted Krystal's hand. "Ah, yes. I saw him head off down the hall." She shared a look with Oren. "Don't worry. They can be a little... strange about protecting their women."

Krystal's eyebrows shot up so fast they were in danger of joining her hair. "What?"

Oren grumbled something and scowled before leaving the room, heading after T'arq.

Krystal struggled to sit up in bed. "What is going on?"

Amelia reached to help her adjust the bed so she could sit. "Why don't you tell me what you remember, hmm?" Her blue eyes were warm as she smiled at Krystal and went some way to calming her racing heart.

"We were testing the cloak, just the two of us," she started. "Things went to shit and the last I knew I was about to asphyxiate, T'arq had knocked himself out and was attached to an alien ship, and I had just risked my life on a wish and a prayer for rescue."

Amelia laughed, and pulling the chair closer to the bed, sat down. She handed Krystal a cup of water. "Sounds like one hell of a date."

Krystal had barely taken a sip before she spat the water out, coughing. "What?"

Amelia handed her a napkin. "That man doesn't get worked up over anyone or anything, Krystal."

"Oh." She twisted the napkin in her hands, not sure what to do with that piece of information. A change of subject seemed the best bet. "How did you find us?"

"A bit of luck and a lot of skill on Oren's part." Amelia settled back in her chair.

Krystal's eyes widened.

"Oren and I were on a... humanitarian mission, I suppose you would call it."

"That's fortunate for us." Krystal figured that, much like

speaking with Laila, it would do no good trying to get more details from Amelia. "I don't know what to say."

"Thank you would do." Amelia grinned. "You're lucky Oren and I were close enough to pick up your distress beacon. There was a lot of interference going on around that asteroid field."

She had come so close to dying. She shuddered. "It was really that close?"

"Mmm." The doctor tilted her head to one side. "Another few minutes and you would have suffocated, going by the amount of oxygen left in those tanks."

"And T'arq?"

"Sub-Commander Qu'Ress?" Amelia smirked at the blush that spread across Krystal's cheeks. "Oh, I'm sure he's been in stickier situations than this."

"What?"

The doctor leaned back in the chair; head tilted to one side as she considered Krystal. "How much do you know about what he does?"

Krystal frowned. "He's a pilot."

Amelia raised an eyebrow, and Krystal ran over all that she knew about T'arq. Yes, he was a pilot, but how many would take direct orders from a starship captain? And he was always with Zac and Laila, and never socialized with the other pilots. In fact, she had only ever seen him in the all ranks bar. Maybe all that snooping had done her some good, after all.

"There's more than that, isn't there?" Krystal pushed herself upright, swinging her legs over the side of the bed. Amelia was immediately at her side, steadying her with a hand at her elbow.

"Easy. You might feel light-headed. Take some big breaths for me."

Following the instruction, Krystal fought the black spots that swum across her vision. She thought she had seen the real T'arq; the kind and caring man who took the time to learn her favorite color and program a replicator to create a flight suit to fit her perfectly. She smoothed a hand down the deep purple suit.

"You might also want to ask him about those eyes of his."

"His eyes?" What did T'arq's eyes have to do with anything? "I know they're unusual, but he is an alien."

Amelia smiled grimly. "Taureans don't have purple eyes, Krystal."

Had it all been a ruse? How much was the real T'arq and how much was a cover for... well, what exactly? If she was to believe what Amelia was saying, then there was a lot she didn't know.

She lifted her head and met the other woman's pale blue eyes. "I need to speak with him."

———

The shuttle was too small to have a bridge like a starship, but big enough to have sleeping quarters, the tiny medical bay where she'd woken up, a cargo hold, and a galley. It was in the galley that she found T'arq, slumped over a steaming cup of coffee.

He looked up as soon as she entered the cramped space, his face wary and closed as if he expected admonishment from her. He pushed to his feet and rounded the small table where he sat. "Coffee?"

"Please." The wary politeness hung thick in the air.

Krystal sat at the table, across from where T'arq's mug sent spirals of steam into the cool galley. The seats were Taurean sized, like everything she had come across, and Krystal had to heave herself up to sit and, instead of letting her feet dangle, she tucked them up underneath her.

T'arq turned after filling her cup from the carafe tucked behind a clear, sealed door. He caught her puzzled look. "It prevents spills."

"Oh." That made sense. The more that Krystal learned about the practical side of Taurean inventions, the more she felt at home here. Or had.

"So—" T'arq began, sliding the mug toward her.

"I—" Krystal said at the same time.

They both laughed nervously, the tension diffusing a little.

"You go first," Krystal offered.

T'arq wrapped his hands around the mug, flexing his broad fingers as he stared into the dark liquid. He opened his mouth as if to speak, but shook his head and took a sip instead. He avoided her eyes as he put the mug down, looking everywhere but at her.

"You were right."

"About what?"

He finally looked at her, his lilac eyes sad pools. "I got you into this."

Krystal picked up her coffee mug and breathed in the familiar aroma. It smelled divine. Thankfully. There were few things worse in this galaxy than awful coffee. She took a long sip, savoring the flavor of the drink before swallowing and carefully placing her mug back on the table. "No. I got me into this."

He shook his head. "You said it yourself. You wouldn't be here if it wasn't for me."

That was true, yes, but had he misunderstood her completely? "Yes, T'arq, but—"

He scowled. "Krystal, I almost got you killed. I sent you on a one-way spacewalk. The chances of you coming out of that alive were slim to fucking none!"

She paled, but her gaze held steady. "It was my choice to come on the test flight."

He ran a hand over his hair, sending blonde curls in every direction. "I couldn't live with myself if anything happened to you." His voice was barely above a whisper.

"T'arq, look at me." She ducked her head to meet his reluctant gaze. "Where are we right now?"

He looked puzzled, but checked his comm. "In the galley of a shuttle, about thirty minutes from the Zataras."

"Exactly." She sat back against the seat, one leg up on the seat and an arm looped casually around her knee.

"I'm not anywhere near your mental capabilities, but I'm usually not this dense. Fill me in?"

She smiled, glad to see a little of the T'arq she knew and... no, don't go there. A little of the T'arq she knew. "Would the me of yesterday have been here like this?" She gestured at her casual pose.

"No." T'arq frowned and shook his head.

"And why is that?"

"I know what you're trying to do, Krystal. I'm still to blame. Zac specifically told me to keep you safe."

Krystal's smile fell, and she dropped the casual pose,

sitting stiffly on the seat. "I knew it," she said under her breath, sliding from the seat. "You're just the same as everyone else. Why can't you let me make my own decisions? I'm a grown adult!" She pointed a finger at him. "Or was it a game? I know you were bored. Hours and hours of flying in straight lines so the nerd can collect her data. Fun times, right? What's a little game to amuse yourself when you're used to much more... sophisticated entertainment?"

T'arq slid from his seat to stand next to her. "What are you talking about?"

"What do you really do, T'arq?"

He shot her a puzzled look. "What? I'm a pilot."

"Sure. And pilots can afford trips to Irith's Moons."

He held out a hand, palm up. "I broke down and needed somewhere to stop."

She wished he hadn't said that. The thing is, Krystal had access to all the engineering logs and, being a stickler for safety, had checked all the maintenance logs on the stealth ship before she had set foot near it. There had been no repairs done on Irith's Moons. When T'arq had returned, the ship had been checked over thoroughly. Krystal had read the reports herself. There had been no breakdown.

He was lying. And there was nothing she hated more than lies.

"You're lying." She leveled a gaze at him. "Who are you, really?" Her stomach flopped as she waited for his answer. A sense of heavy expectation hung between them, as if his next words were the most important he had ever said. As if they would decide something monumental.

He swallowed, his throat bobbing before he spoke. "I don't know how to answer that."

Krystal sniffed in disgust and turned on her heel, ready to leave the room, not able to look at him for one second longer.

"Krystal—" T'arq began, but his comm buzzed, Oren calling him to the cockpit. "Can we talk later?" he asked, his eyes pleading with her.

"We have nothing more to say to each other," She replied, turning away to dump her coffee in what she hoped was a sink, unable to stomach the bitter brew.

He sighed and left without argument, which stung more than it should.

Alone, she slid back onto the bench and lay her head on the table on her pillowed arms. She bit back a sob. How had she become so invested in him in such a short amount of time? Laila had warned her about him, and she hadn't listened. She had been so stupid and should have known better. She had seen the people he favored, women and men alike. They all fit the same mold—tall, sensual in a way Krystal could never hope to be, and sophisticated. The exact opposite of short, clumsy and girl next door Krystal.

Ugh.

She banged her head on the table.

"That good, huh?"

She lifted her head to see Amelia in the doorway. She dropped her head back into her hands.

"We're about to dock with the Zataras."

The two women made their way to the cockpit, where Oren and T'arq sat in front of the controls, guiding the ship toward the gaping maw of the shuttle bay. They sat in two jump seats that folded down in the cramped space behind the main seats and buckled in. Not that there was any need. Krystal watched as T'arq skillfully guided the shuttle in to land, the looming expanse of the Zataras reassuringly familiar as it enveloped them. The shuttle hovered above the indicated bay before rotating gently to set down, landing feet extended.

The entire process had taken less than a minute.

Krystal's fingers bit into the edge of the seat and she forced them to flex as she breathed out a hard breath.

"Krystal?" T'arq's voice was concerned as he turned in his seat to look at her. The other two had already unbuckled and had left the cockpit.

"I'm fine." She fiddled with the clasp, shaking fingers unable to hit the latch. "Fuck!"

"Hey. It's ok. I've got you." T'arq was right there, at her side, skilled fingers releasing the catch and lifting her from the seat.

She stiffened against him. "You can let me down now."

He did immediately, letting go and stepping back. "I'm sorry." His eyes seemed to plead with her to understand.

To understand what? He had lied to her.

She pressed her lips together and shook her head, turning away to follow Amelia and Oren from the shuttle. They walked down the ramp and onto the shuttle bay floor to a small welcoming party. Domik greeted his brother Oren with the close head touch of friends before bowing low to Amelia. The doctor shot a confused look at Oren, who laughed, shaking his head and pushing his brother lightly on the shoulder.

Laila rushed toward her and threw her arms around Krystal, Zac following closely behind her. Krystal extracted herself from her sister's embrace and took a step backwards. "I'm fine, Laila. Really."

The difference between the two was striking. Laila was tall, where Krystal was short. Laila was Amazonian in her stature, where Krystal was what she would call dumpy on a bad day and curvy when she was feeling generous. Laila walked with a confident stride, a woman who knew her place in the world. Krystal carried a step stool.

Laila grasped her by the shoulders and looked down into her upturned face. "Really? Because we both know how you feel about—"

"I said I'm fine." Krystal forced a smile. "Really, I am."

"Why do I not believe you?"

"If she said she's fine, then she's fine." T'arq almost growled.

Krystal stiffened, the heat of his body on her back making her acutely aware of just how close he was standing. She whirled to face him, her eyes hitting him smack in the middle of his chest.

His very broad chest.

She stumbled, taking a step backwards, and his hand shot out to steady her with a gentle but firm grip on her elbow. Her skin burned with the touch of his fingers and she jerked out of his grasp. He wouldn't tell her the truth, but he hovered over her like it was his right to be her protector? She shook with anger at his presumption.

Zac spoke to Krystal. "Your cloak was so successful that the Supreme Commander himself wants to talk to you about it."

"What?" Both Krystal and T'arq spoke in unison. She felt his eyes on her, but refused to look at him.

What would the leader of the Taurean people want with her? Just one small piece of technology. One small piece of technology that had not been as successful as they seemed to think. The Xakul drone had found them, after all. And she was still trying to puzzle out how that had happened. And she was still so annoyed with T'arq that she couldn't think straight.

Krystal swallowed; her mouth as dry as a desert. "When?" She choked out.

"Right now." Zac's expression was grim.

Shit. She paled.

"Both of you." Zac gestured to her and T'arq. "Now."

She shot a look at T'arq, whose normally golden skin had paled, his hands in fists by his side.

Double shit.

CHAPTER FIFTEEN

T'arq

T'arq stalked through the corridors of the Zataras, barely registering the people who greeted him as he passed.

Shit. Shit. Shit.

He clenched and unclenched his fists as he walked. She wouldn't talk to him, and what would he say, anyway?

I'm sorry I lied?

He was sorry that he had lied, but admitting that he had lied would mean needing to tell the truth. He could hardly apologize for lying and then turn around and not tell her why. Scoffing at the thought that she would let him get away with that. Like hell she would.

What else could he say? Nothing. That's what was expected of him, wasn't it? The playboy who just dallied in superficial flings. The promiscuous warrior with the reputation as an insatiable lover. He'd never cared what people thought of him before, but now? He wanted Krystal to know who he really was, deep down and not the person he let others see.

She had seen past the facade, and he'd been given a taste of connection. He craved it like a dying man in a desert craving water. Was this what he had been missing all along?

No.

He stopped in the middle of the hallway, a cadet almost crashing into him but dodging at the last minute to thump into the wall. "Sorry, Sub-Commander!" the young Taurean said, eyes wide as he backed away from T'arq.

Was he really that frightening? He looked down at himself and brushed at his uniform with his hand, suddenly self-conscious in his filthy and torn flight suit as he stood in the pristine hallway. He had left oily footprints that a cleaner bot was scrubbing at, the little bot the same model as the one Krystal had been repairing yesterday.

Was it only yesterday?

He ran a hand over his face and sighed. It felt like a lifetime ago.

He began walking again, turning down the corridor that would take him to the bridge. His torn flight suit flapped around his ankles, the rent in the leg opening one side from ankle to thigh, gusts of cold air from the floor vents blasting his legs above his combat boots.

He should have been able to prevent this. He'd promised Krystal she would be safe. And she hadn't been. He'd known following the Xakul was dangerous, and he'd done it, anyway. He deserved every bit of her anger and distrust. His lips thinned as he thought, once again, about how he had almost cost her life.

He'd wanted her to see him for who he was and what had

he shown her? The exact opposite. He dragged a hand through his hair, sending the already messy strands into complete disarray. He'd kissed her when he knew she wanted more than he could offer. Hadn't she said as much? And he, in all his ego, had what? Had he thought it was a challenge?

His stomach turned, and he swallowed bile.

It was one thing to not want to get involved with someone too closely, but he always made sure the people he slept with felt the same way. He knew getting too closely involved would be trouble. He knew that wasn't what she was like.

And still he had kissed her.

T'arq forced his jaw to relax from where it was clenched. There was only one thing for it—he had to stay away from Krystal. Even if she forgave him for lying—and he doubted she would—he wasn't made for deep feelings and relationships. One night, maybe two, that was it. But a lifetime?

He scoffed, feeling an uncomfortable burn in his chest. Was the thought of a lifetime with Krystal so bad? He dodged the thought. She wouldn't even talk to him now, so why even think about it?

Even so, the little whispered thought persisted.

Realizing he had reached the door to the bridge, T'arq stopped and looked down at himself and his torn and stained uniform. He must be a sight. There was nothing for it but to get this over with. He swiped his wrist over the scanner pad.

The door opened to reveal the bridge. A Taurean starship's bridge was adaptable to the activity and the captain. The room's walls were lined with interactive viewscreen panels, three currently showing the view outside the big starship. As they were on alert for attack by the Xakul, the bridge had been configured for combat.

The Zataras' bridge was a hive of activity. Workers were busy tapping on their interactive panels for their designated tasks, some seated and some standing. And in the center of it all was where Tomas Ka'Ress would stand.

No big comfortable seat for him. A pilot originally, he preferred to stand and only strapped himself into the co-pilot's seat when things really got rough. Right now, he was leaning over the shoulder of one of the ship's tactical officers. The two were deep in conversation, their voices inaudible. Tomas straightened and clapped the other man on the shoulder, smiling at him before turning to face T'arq.

His smile dropped. T'arq knew Tomas as Zac's cousin, but when in his own territory, then he was entirely the starship captain, and not the friendly cousin. His face was pure Taurean upper-class elegance. High cheekbones and a powerful jaw were the backdrop to a face with the same piercing green eyes that Zac had. Not for him was the telling purple of T'arq's eyes.

He turned and gestured for T'arq to follow him, crossing to a door on the other side of the bridge. T'arq followed, entering a room with a large table around which humans and Taureans sat.

"You're late." Zac did not stand, and by his curt tone was obviously displeased with his friend.

T'arq nodded, taking the only empty seat, which was next to Krystal. "I walked."

Whatever this was about, he was going to take the brunt of any fallout. Krystal didn't deserve to be hauled over the coals for just trying to make things better. It was T'arq who lost the stealth ship. T'arq who had drawn the attention of the Xakul. T'arq, who had almost gotten them killed.

"The transporter would have been quicker."

T'arq bit back angry words and nodded at his friend and commander. He braced his hands on the arms of the chair. He was angry with himself, not at Zac. And not at Krystal. He needed to apologize to her.

T'arq turned. "Krystal—"

"The Supreme Commander is on screen." Tomas swiped at his comm and the screen that took up the entire wall at the end of the table flickered into life.

T'arq had missed it coming into the room, so fixated was he on Krystal. She was in a similar state to him, neither of them having time to change, but she had restrained her hair. She stared straight ahead instead of looking past him to the viewscreen.

Squaring his shoulders, he tensed, hands braced on the table in front of him, and waited for whatever was going to be thrown their way.

He forced himself to look at the viewscreen as the image of the Supreme Commander flickered into life. He was lounging in a large padded chair, one leg thrown over the armrest, his hand dangling as he looked at something off-screen and laughed. The size of the view screen made him look twice as large as he was in real life.

Karik Za'Rell was an infamous layabout, known for his over the top parties and excessive spending on the most frivolous of things. What he was not known for was his interest in military matters. Would Krystal see more in this man than the carefully cultivated facade? A facade so good that T'arq still struggled to accept it was fake.

But she wasn't looking at the viewscreen, or T'arq. She was looking at the tablet in front of her on the table. T'arq craned his neck to read it, but she must have felt him doing so and tucked it away before shooting him a glare.

Obviously not forgiven... yet. He eased back into his seat and turned to watch the view screen once more.

Karik Za'Rell had not been the first choice for Supreme Commander. Or the second. And, according to palace gossip, probably not even the third. But his father had held the role before him and his elder brother had been groomed to ascend to the throne at their father's death. According to Taurean tradition, Karik had not even had the same surname as his father and elder brother, instead, his surname had been equal parts of his mother's and father's surnames. Until his older brother's death had meant Karik had become the new heir.

A tradition that T'arq would be glad to see disappear, but many were in disagreement, the Taurean Purists most of all.

It wasn't only the Xakul that were a threat to humans. T'arq shot a look at Krystal, fingers biting into the flesh of his thighs at the thought of her getting into the hands of the secret organization that had sprung out of nowhere.

He did not envy Karik Za'Rell. Not one bit.

But that still didn't answer the question that had been bugging T'arq. Why now? What did Karik Za'Rell want?

"Supreme Commander, Sir," Zac said, and Karik Za'Rell finally turned to look at them through the viewscreen, a lazy smile on his face.

"Zac," he drawled, "do we really need all these people here?" He gestured with a hand, dropping it by his side as he, once again, looked off-screen.

T'arq watched as Zac nodded, directing all but Tomas, Laila, Krystal, and himself to leave the room. When the door had shut behind the last, Zac turned back to the screen. "As you requested, sir."

Karik's posture changed instantly. The indolent sprawl disappeared, his eyes no longer sliding off-screen. He smoothed his hair back from his forehead and sat upright in the chair, reaching for a tablet, and flicking through the pages with ruthless efficiency.

If he hadn't seen the change himself, T'arq would have thought this was a different person.

"What have I said about calling me that?" Karik said, head still lowered but eyes lifted and an eyebrow raised.

Zac chuckled. "Old habits..."

"Yeah, yeah. Laila, are you keeping him in line?"

"Always." Zac scowled at Laila, fighting to look stern as she grinned at him.

"So, this cloak...? Tell me about it." Karik sat back in his seat, elbows resting on the armrests and fingers steepled together.

Silence filled the room.

"That would be you, Krystal," T'arq said quietly.

She jolted in her seat. "Me?"

"Yes, you."

Their eyes met, and T'arq smiled gently, hoping to send some reassurance to her. She looked away quickly.

He sighed.

"Sir...?" Krystal began, her voice cracking on the word. She cleared her throat, continuing more confidently. "The cloak is a modification of your previous technology..."

The details were quickly lost on T'arq and, instead; he

watched as she waved her hands enthusiastically. All she wanted was to be of use, to help people in some small way. And she had, except for that minor issue with the drone sensing them, but he was confident she would sort that out. She had sorted everything else out, hadn't she? He felt a warm wash of pride fill him as he watched her speak. Her face was so expressive—her passion clear. What would it feel like to be the object of such adoration? A sudden craving hit him for her to look at him with the same passion she had for her work.

"... and T'arq."

"Huh?" He jolted in his seat, blinking and looking around the room.

Laila's eyes narrowed, and she began to speak, but stopped as Zac touched her arm lightly.

"Not now," he said, and she pressed her lips together in obvious disagreement.

T'arq turned to look at Krystal, who took an unsteady breath and shuddered.

"Krystal?" He ducked his head to catch her eyes, but she avoided looking at him, turning her head, a slight flush filling her cheeks.

"Sub-Commander Qu'Ress," Karik's voice had him turning sharply to address the Supreme Commander.

"Yes, sir?"

Karik rolled his eyes. "It's never going to stop, is it?" He spoke to someone off-camera that T'arq couldn't see. A light laugh and a mumbled reply came and Karik grinned, then turned back to T'arq. "You have obviously been focusing on someone much more important than me," he said, an eyebrow cocked in question.

He glanced at Krystal, whose face had gotten even more red. Something in her lap was fascinating, though, as she wouldn't look anywhere else.

He sighed, running a hand over his face. "I'm sure I don't know what you mean. *Sir*," he said, unable to stop the note of challenge in his voice.

To his surprise, the most powerful man in the entire Taurean empire threw his head back and laughed. "What is it with you warrior types and humans, hey?"

Zac grunted, Laila choked, and Krystal finally looked up from her lap.

"Specialist Storey will—"

"*Specialist* Storey?" T'arq interjected.

"You really weren't listening, were you?" Zac shot him a look. T'arq shrugged. "Karik offered Krystal a role as the fleet's cloaking specialist."

T'arq gaped, then quickly darted a look at the woman next to him. "Are you going to accept?"

Her usually transparent expression was unreadable. "What do you think?"

And wasn't that the problem? He hadn't been thinking. He'd been feeling, and look where that had gotten him—all tied up in knots. He knew better than that. Don't get involved. Never get involved.

Too late.

"Specialist Storey will roll out the cloak upgrades fleet wide," Zac explained, "and you are going to help her. As the only pilot who has flown a ship with this new cloak, it makes perfect sense."

T'arq grunted. Even if it made little sense, he could hardly reject a direct order.

Karik cleared his throat, drawing the attention of all in the room once more. "Then there is the matter of this new Xakul threat."

Tomas stood and, flicking a second view screen into life, scrolled through images that T'arq had taken of the Xakul mass. Had Krystal saved the data drive from the stealth ship as well?

"They have to be destroyed. We cannot have such a large force massing so close to the only human settlements. If they reach Earth..."

Nobody spoke, though their grim faces said enough.

"The cloak's not ready," Krystal spoke up. "I can't put troops in danger like that." She sat back, arms crossed over her chest, as if daring anyone to question her.

T'arq suppressed a smile, a warm wash of pride filling him as he watched her square off against not only her only family, but the captain of a Taurean starship.

"I'm sure—" Laila began.

Krystal cut her off. "You don't know. You weren't there!" She turned to face T'arq, eyes pleading with him to help. "Tell them, T'arq! I can't put more people in danger."

T'arq held her gaze, eyes roving over her face. As if he could refuse her anything. He turned to look address Zac. "She needs to know."

Zac's eyes met his as he nodded. "I'd been thinking the same thing myself."

Laila sat upright in her seat, slapping a hand on the table. "What? No. She's—"

"I'm what, Laila? A kid? Too young? Do you really want to finish that sentence, because I am done with you," she gestured around the table, "thinking you can decide for me!" She stood, her chair falling backwards in her haste.

"Sit down," Karik said, though his words were warm and a small grin tilted his lips. He raised his hands in surrender with a chuckle.

"What?" Krystal whispered, finally looking at T'arq, who helped right her chair as she sat back down.

He smiled and nodded, whispering, "I lied because I had no choice. I'm sorry."

Her eyes widened. "What?"

"Do you know what we do, Krystal?" Zac asked, waving a hand to include the group seated at the table.

"I know you do more than what you've told me. There's no reason for an advisor," she inclined her head to indicate Laila, "and a troop trainer," she nodded toward Zac, "to be gallivanting all over the place. At least not together." She scoffed.

Karik laughed and then quickly brought Krystal up to speed with the purpose of the team of humans and Taureans. "So, we want you to be attached to the team."

"Oh," Krystal managed, her mouth dropping open, eyes skipping over first Laila, then Zac and finally resting on T'arq.

"Do you accept?" Laila asked, leaning forward across the table.

"Yes, of course," Krystal said, eyes darting back to her sister.

"Good. The first thing is to get that cloak sorted," Karik said.

"I still feel the cloak's not ready," she said.

"She's right. If we send ships out without a working cloak,

the Xakul response will be swift and, unfortunately, predictable," T'arq agreed.

A gasp from next to him made him glance back at the little human engineer.

"You're a genius!" She exclaimed, clapping her hands together before pushing back from the table and racing for the door.

She disappeared, leaving a stunned silence in her wake. T'arq and Zac looked at Laila, who shrugged. "She'll be—" Laila was cut off by Krystal dashing back into the room, hands grabbing the door frame as her hair whipped wildly around her face.

"Sorry! I know how to fix it. Give me a few hours?" she said, before disappearing through the door once more.

T'arq burst into laughter, shaking his head. "Once she gets an idea..."

CHAPTER SIXTEEN

Krystal

He was a genius! Well, maybe not, but he'd said that one thing that had made her realize how to fix the problem with the cloak.

The Xakul response would be predictable.

It all hinged on the cloak being predictable. The coding she had used cycled through a complex sequence but, given enough effort, it was predictable. It was that exact predictability that had caused the problems. So the way to fix it was to make it unpredictable.

Easier said than done.

She had rushed from the meeting and immediately got to work, holing herself up in her small room. She was currently curled up in the single armchair that, along with the narrow bed, took up most of the space. Well, it was narrow by Taurean standards, but felt like a luxury to Krystal.

Civilian rooms on a Taurean starship were not glamorous, but they were functional. At least she had her own bathroom, which was better than the small apartment she had shared with a colleague back on Earth. Krystal had taken the time to shower as soon as she got back to her room, and had been working ever since.

She sighed and rubbed her temples. A certain Taurean warrior's face kept appearing every time she closed her eyes. She had been so angry with him, but now? Now she knew he had lied because he'd had no other choice.

Krystal had just finished the final tweaks to the coding when her comm buzzed.

She checked the time, realizing with a shock that it was the middle of the night. Six hours? She had been working for six hours straight? She rolled her shoulders, easing the stiffness and stretching her arms over her head.

A little bit of time had helped her realize a few things. T'arq hadn't lied. Not really. He had omitted part of the truth, skirting the actual issue, but he had tried to tell her as much as he could. She wasn't upset with him for that. She was still annoyed that he was trying to decide for her, though.

The comm buzzed again.

"Yes?" Krystal answered.

The voice that spilled through the small speaker had her swallowing nervously. "Are you done?" T'arq asked.

"Yes," she croaked. She coughed and reached for the glass on the small side table, taking a large swig.

"Good. Open the door."

She choked on the water, barely swallowing. He was outside her room? Now? She had been so eager to get to work that she hadn't even dressed properly after her shower, just pulling on panties and a tank top before wrapping herself up in a blanket.

"Uh..." Her brain—her useless brain—would not come up with anything to say. She cursed.

"Now, Krystal."

Oh, no. Krystal untangled her legs from a blanket she had wrapped around herself, managing to not trip over the trailing end, and headed to the door.

"What are you doing here?" she asked when it opened, trying to wrap the blanket around her more securely and only exposing her shoulder. Her very bare shoulder.

His gaze traveled over her, taking in her disheveled hair, the blanket barely covering her almost naked form, her bare feet.

"Are you alone?" His eyes were an intense purple, flashing lilac with the beat of his heart. Fast. Hypnotic. She'd never seen anything like it.

"What?"

"Are. You. Alone," he ground out, looking past her into the room.

Krystal turned around to see what he was looking at. The room was a mess. The bed had not been made since before they had left on the stealth ship. There were clothes on the floor, and she had accumulated a small army of drinking glasses. She had every intention of taking them back to the mess, but she just never remembered. As she turned, the blanket slipped down her shoulders to expose her back and she frantically grabbed at the tail end, instead dropping the entire thing.

An animal growl escaped through T'arq's clenched teeth, his breath coming in hard pants. She dropped to her knees to pick up the blanket and gasped when a huge, heavy hand landed on her shoulder and squeezed ever so gently, but ever so insistently.

If anyone saw them... this was not a good position to be caught in.

"T'arq?" she asked, annoyed that her voice sounded breathy and needy.

She tried to stand, but his hand held her still, on her knees before him. She stared up at him, head tilted back, her hands reaching to steady herself against his legs. His thick, strong, muscular thighs flexed under her fingers as if she had branded him. She focused on the straining length of his cock that was close enough that she could lean forward and... she swayed toward him, her eyelids dropping half-closed. Was that her moaning? Surely not.

One second she was on her knees before him, the next she was in his muscular arms and, with a handful of steps, tossed onto her bed where she bounced.

"Hey!"

The door slid shut. She panted, breaths coming fast as she watched him standing at the end of the bed, looming over her.

"Your eyes..." she whispered.

"What about them?" His voice was deeper than she had ever heard it.

"They're changing colors."

He grunted in reply before easing a knee onto the bed and dropping to all fours to crawl toward her, agonizingly slowly. "You are a siren." One arm moved closer, his hand near her knee. "A temptress." The other hand moved to the bed near her hip as her legs fell open of their own accord.

"Your hips are made for my hands to hold as I slide into your slick heat."

She whimpered as his other hand moved to cage her in between his chest and the bed, but still he didn't touch her. "Your breasts for my lips to worship." He eased closer, his chest so close to her that if she arched off the bed, they would touch. "Your mouth," his head dropped to the side of her neck, his hot breath sending shivers through her, "is made for me to devour."

Krystal couldn't take it any longer. With every sinuous movement of his body over hers, with every word she had flooded with arousal. She had never been so turned on in her life. She arched up to press herself against him, her arms wrapping around his neck.

"Do not misunderstand my intentions, Krystal. The things I want to do to you." He groaned, pulling his head back when she would have kissed him. "I want you in the most depraved ways."

Krystal whined in frustration. She actually whined. "I want this. I want you."

T'arq's smile was predatory as he looked down at her. He pulled his bottom lip between his teeth, eyes flashing an even darker purple. "Tell me what you want from me, little mouse."

"I want you," she pleaded, winding her fingers through his hair. The locks were longer than when she had first met him, and she enjoyed the feeling of the soft strands on her fingers.

"No." His voice deepened as he drew out the word.

Her fingers stilled; brows drawn together in confusion. "No?"

"Tell me *exactly* what you want from me."

"Oh." She flushed bright red. She could feel the color spreading over her. "I can't." She whispered, looking away, and drawing her hands back from where they had rested around his neck.

Long fingers gripped her chin firmly to turn her face to look at him. "If you can't ask, you get nothing."

Krystal wriggled, desperately seeking... something... trying to push herself against him. T'arq took her hands above her head and held them against the mattress in one big hand.

"Tell me."

Panting, she writhed on the bed underneath him and whispered. "I want you... to... fuck me."

"Louder."

She cleared her throat. "I want you to fuck me."

"You can do better than that, little mouse. Look at me."

Thankful that the rooms were well insulated against noise, Krystal let loose. "I want you to fuck me!" She finally managed a volume that met with his approval.

"Good girl." He purred, sliding one hand down her neck to gently caress the dip of her waist. She didn't think she could get any more turned on, but at his words she whimpered, heat pooling low in her belly.

"What do you want first?" He smirked, obviously enjoying himself immensely.

"I want you naked." She tried to hide her face as she spoke.

He laughed. "Whatever you wish, little mouse." He eased himself away from her and she felt the loss immediately, reaching to cover herself with her hands. "Don't," he said, and she let her hands drop away to lie sprawled on the messy bed covers in just her briefs and tank top. That had cartoon animals on them. Again. He didn't seem bothered by that, thankfully.

She watched, transfixed, as he straightened to stand by the bed. He stared at her intently, his expression serious, breath coming in deep pulls. She shifted on the bed and he jerked a hand to stop her.

"Be still," he barked, and she froze. Although his tone was harsh, there was a tilt to his lips, and she was not afraid.

The tip of her tongue darted out to wet her lips, and he groaned. "That tongue of yours is going to do all sorts of things to me." He gripped the zipper at the top of his flight suit, a different one to what he had worn before, she noted absently.

"That's a new flight suit."

He lifted an eyebrow. "As if I would bring myself anywhere near you without being clean."

She watched, transfixed, as his hand slowly drove the zipper downwards, the teeth unclenching to open, displaying his broad, well-muscled chest beneath. His skin was a deep bronze in some places and golden in others.

"Everywhere your eyes touch me, you will kiss me," he purred.

She rubbed her thighs together, trying to get some relief.

"Did I say you could move?"

She shook her head and froze.

"So stay still."

She nodded, watching the hand that had stopped, the zipper pull now just below his navel. She almost choked as the muscles of his flat stomach were revealed. Was that an eight pack? Who had one of those?

"Where will you kiss me?" His voice was deeper, each word spoken slowly as if they had all the time in the universe.

"Everywhere," she whispered, willing his hand to just move. She wanted to scream with frustration as he let the zipper pull go and spread his hands wide.

"Do you like what you see, Krystal?" He grinned and winked at her.

"Take it off," she demanded, meeting his eyes briefly before focusing again at that tantalizing glimpse of abdomen.

He didn't move.

"Please, T'arq."

"Since you asked so nicely," he said, turning his back on her and pulling his arms from the flight suit, the one-piece garment slithering down his torso, stopping its descent at his hips. The muscles in his back bunched as he moved unhurriedly.

She groaned in frustration, and he shot a look at her over his shoulder. Dear God, this man would be the end of her!

"Is this what you wanted?"

"No."

He lifted the suit back up as if to shrug back into it.

"Stop! You know what I mean. Take it off, please. You're killing me!" She gave in and slipped a hand between her legs under her panties, desperately seeking the satisfaction she craved. She rolled her fingers over her clit, just the way she liked it.

"Krystal." The word was uttered on a growl and her eyes flew open—when had she shut them—to see T'arq staring at her over his shoulder with a frown. Shit.

She whipped her hand out of her pants. "Sorry."

"You will be."

Oh boy. If one could die of sexual frustration, then that was the way she would surely go.

Still standing with his back to her, his hand moved in front of him and she itched to see what he was doing, but dared not move again. She strained to hear, but her pulse was so loud in her ears it made no difference.

His flight suit slid a little lower, catching on the swell of his muscular backside. He spread his legs a little wider, and the suit slipped down his legs to catch on the tops of his thighs.

Fuck. That was one hell of an ass.

He kicked free of the legs of the flight suit, stepping out of the garment, so he stood naked in front of her. When had he taken his boots off? More importantly, what was he doing with his hands?

Krystal lay still, hardly daring to breathe as she watched him slowly turn to face her. She drank in the sight of him. Ridges and shallows, valleys and mountains of muscle and silky skin that were meant for exploration.

And, boy, did she want to explore.

As he turned to face her fully, her breath caught in her throat. One big hand was cupping the heavy sac that nestled between his muscular thighs, squeezing and rolling their delicate contents. The other was lazily stroking the absolute biggest monster of a cock she had ever seen.

Holy shit. How? Where?

She swallowed as she followed the movement of his hand. Up, squeeze, a twist and flick, release, down... and then repeated. Slow passes of his hand that had her wanting to see if she could make him feel just as good.

"Remember what I said?"

"Hmm?" She couldn't remember her name, let alone what he had said.

"Everywhere your eyes touch me, you will kiss me." Each word was spoken as a promise.

"Yes, please."

He smirked. "Come here."

She bolted upright and scrambled across the bed toward him. He chuckled, gesturing for her to sit on the edge of the bed, which put her head at the perfect height to say hello to his not so little friend. She reached forward, but he batted her hands away gently.

"Not so fast, little mouse. Lie down," he said with a gentle push to the middle of her chest. When she complied, he dropped to his knees in front of her and gripped the sides of her panties. "What are these?"

"My underwear?"

"No, these," he said, running a finger over the fabric.

She lifted her head to look and dropped it back with a giggle, and threw an arm over her face. "They're kittens."

"My translator says that is a baby feline?"

"Yes."

"Why...?"

"They're cute, and I like baby animals." She was having a conversation about cartoon kittens on her underwear while the hottest man... alien... was naked and between her legs? Who was she and what had happened to Krystal Storey?

"I like your cat."

Wait. What?

"What?"

"Your cat," he said, gripping the sides of her panties and sliding them down her legs, exposing her core to his fiery gaze.

"My what?" She blinked rapidly.

He pulled her panties free and flung them over his shoulder to land who knew where, then slid his hands up the insides of her legs to push her thighs apart. He pushed her knees back until they hit her chest. "Hold your legs like this."

A moment of panic at being so open, rushed over her, but it was gone the next instant as he spread her open with his thumbs and stroked her, spreading her sopping wet arousal over her lips.

"Your cat."

She burst into laughter, which was quickly stifled as he dipped his head and licked her like she was the most delicious delicacy and he was a starving man.

"You mean my pussy," she gasped as he found her clit with his tongue and flicked little circles around it.

He hummed as he sucked her clit into his mouth and tugged gently. She felt her legs go weak and she let go of her legs as the world narrowed to T'arq and what he was doing to her *pussy*.

Fuck. This was the most pleasure she had ever experienced.

And then he slid a thick finger into her and curled it in just the most perfect way and she exploded.

CHAPTER SEVENTEEN

T'arq

S he tasted like the sweetest flower wine from Taurus' most exclusive vineyards. Like rain after a drought. Like Krystal.

She tasted like home.

Her back arched and her eyes closed as she came, her perfect mouth making gasping and her neat teeth gripping her bottom lip. He was lost.

She whimpered as wave after wave of pleasure washed over her and he knew he would never want for anyone else ever again.

His heart was heavy as he eased his fingers from her.

Don't think about it. Just give her this. It's all you've ever been able to give. Give her what you can and then let her go so she can be happy.

He pushed the thoughts aside as she released a shaky breath.

"Wow," she said, and laughed.

"We're not done yet," he said as he smoothed his hands up her thighs to cup her under her ass. His fingers slid up her back underneath her tank top and pulled it over her head. Her breasts lifted and then dropped, the heavy weight of them filling his palms. He brushed his thumbs over her nipples and dipped his head to capture one between his teeth and gently nip.

"Oh!" Krystal cried out; her head thrown back.

He let go and his hands began a dance across her body, never quite touching where she really wanted, but coming oh so close. Over her hips, between her legs, over her thighs, back over her ass, between her breasts... he worked her skin until she was gasping.

"Now you can kiss me everywhere," he said, straightening to stand in front of her.

He watched as she gathered herself, taking steady breaths and sitting up with her knees dangling over the edge of the bed, her mouth at just the right height that if he lent forward... but no. Make this last.

T'arq held his hands at his side, using all his focus to keep them from moving. He hadn't come here to seduce her. He had come to her room to apologize and ask her forgiveness. For six hours he had paced and practiced and ran words through his head, but as soon as he'd seen her wrapped in that blanket, one shoulder peeking out? He'd been lost.

Who was he kidding? He'd been lost from the beginning.

Her hands touched his thighs, and his focus became Krystal, just her. Only her. Her hands on him, sliding with the lightest of feather touches to slide around and caress the backs of his thighs, and slide upwards over the curve of his ass. His abdomen tensed, his cock bobbing as her face moved closer. She looked up at him hesitantly from under her eyelashes and his heart pounded as if it would burst from his chest.

She was perfect.

She didn't even realize how much of a seductress she was, all curves and biting lips and enormous eyes... and her hair that was a mass of tousled curls flowing around her head like a halo. She was stunning.

She was everything.

And then her mouth closed over him.

His hands moved on their own to fist into her hair and guide her head over his length. Little nibbles down to the base where his dick met the lightly furred skin of his sac.

She pulled away with a gasp. "You have fur?" she asked, her fingers stroking lightly over the sensitive skin.

"Hmm. What did you expect?" He was surprised he formed a sentence, the way her hands moved. Gods.

"I'm not sure. Hair maybe, but this is so silky and short and—" the gods help him, she dropped her mouth down and licked him, "—you taste slightly musky, but in a nice way." She smiled up at him and he fought to keep his knees from buckling.

"Enough," he barked and, hand still fisted in her hair, guided her back to the tip of his cock. She gripped it with both hands and eyed it. "I'll be gentle. Do you trust me?"

She looked up at him and, instead of answering, smiled and licked the head, her tongue seeking the slit and probing before swirling around and her mouth closing around him.

"Hnnng." He lost the ability to form words as he watched her take inch after inch of his cock into her mouth. When she would have taken more, he guided her away, and she moaned around him. She would be the death of him. He just knew it.

She sucked him down again, her hands working his length in slow strokes as her tongue paid homage to him. She had to stretch her lips wide to take his girth, and tears filled her eyes as he watched.

"Too much?"

She shook her head and sucked harder, and he smirked. "Good girl." He ran his hand down her hair, fisting it once more he eased a little more of his cock into her mouth before pulling back out until just the tip rested on her lips. She panted, but leaned forward to take him again. He held her back with his hand in her hair. "Don't be greedy now." She scowled up at him and he chuckled. "This time, try to open a little more for me. Can you do that?" She nodded. "Good girl," he said again, and she opened her mouth for him and looked up expectantly.

"Please. I want you."

He paused, holding the tip of his dick on her lips, his other hand on the back of her head. "Use your words, Krys."

"I want your cock. I want to suck it all down. I want you in me, filling me up." She paused; eyes wide as she stared up at him. "I need you."

He groaned and slid his thick length past her lips. She opened wide for him, taking him deeper than she had before. She wouldn't be able to take him all—he knew that—but watching her try? It was beyond hot. It was scorching.

She swallowed around him and he felt himself slip a little deeper in her throat, tears leaking from her eyes.

He brushed hair back that had fallen over her face. "You're doing so well. That's it, a little more." She swallowed again, her hands dropping from hips to circle around to pull his ass closer to her. T'arq held himself still, careful to not move lest he hurt her, but the need to pump his hips was getting too great. He pulled her head back, and she gasped, pulling needy breaths into her lungs.

Dropping to the mattress next to her, he gathered her in his arms and pressed a kiss to her temple.

"You're a fast learner."

"What can I say? I have a brilliant teacher." She smirked at him, and he dropped his mouth to hers, tasting himself on her. He drew her bottom lip between his teeth and nipped gently, eliciting a gasp from her.

He rolled over, pulling her on top of him, her legs spread on either side of his thighs, and held himself still, eyes roaming over her flushed skin.

"What's wrong?" Her brows drew together.

"Nothing. Just thinking about how perfect you are," he said, sliding a hand around her neck to pull her down for a kiss.

He drowned in her.

Minutes or hours later—who could tell—she lifted her head from his to drop a light kiss on his nose. Something about the movement made his stomach clench.

Her hands roamed over his chest, tracing paths in his skin and following them with her lips before sliding down his sweat-slicked body until she was seated over his hips. She brushed her wet core over his aching cock, holding herself upright with a hand braced against his chest.

His hands circled her waist and lifted her so she was poised over him, her own hands reaching for his cock and lining him up with her entry.

Their eyes met. "Tell me you don't want this and I'll stop right now," he said, though inside he was screaming to thrust up into her hot little body.

"I've never wanted anything more than I want this." Her words were the biggest aphrodisiac. Hands shaking, he eased her down onto his thick length and then stopped.

She made a frustrated mewl and wriggled to pull him deeper.

"Be patient, little mouse." He smirked, though he was barely holding onto his control.

Steadily he slid her down his rigid cock, both of them groaning at the sensation that flooded through them. She was so hot and how she gripped him!

She raised herself and lowered, sinuous movements of her hips, creating a dance that he hoped would be burned into his memories. He never wanted to forget how she braced her hands on her thighs, her back arched and her hair tumbling like water over her shoulders to kiss her bountiful breasts. With each up and down, her curves jiggled enticingly.

Her eyes flew open, and she bit her bottom lip. "Am I a good girl?"

Fuck.

He slid a hand up her back, flattening her to his chest, and rolled her under him, one hand gripping her thigh to keep her impaled on his cock. She was so much shorter than him that her head barely reached his shoulder in this position.

"So fucking good," he groaned as his control snapped and he began pounding into her.

He slid a hand between them to find the tight little

bundle of nerves and circled it with fingers slicked with her arousal. She arched her back and cried out, her pussy walls gripping him as she flew apart.

She cried out words he struggled to understand, but her hands gripping his ass and pulling him closer told him everything he needed to know.

Her orgasm triggered his own, his heavy balls drawing up as he came with a loud growl that sounded more animal than man.

CHAPTER EIGHTEEN

Krystal

When she woke, she was alone. The only sign that she hadn't been dreaming was the ache between her legs. It wasn't unpleasant—not at all—but it was a reminder of what she and T'arq had done. She groaned and stuffed a pillow over her head.

She was so stupid. He turns up on her doorstep and she just, what? Has sex with him? Mind-blowing out of this world —out of this galaxy—sex, sure. But she didn't even ask how he felt about her?

And how could she be annoyed with him deciding for her when he had done exactly that and she had loved every damned second?

She had always thought she wanted what her parents had had. Comfortable and cozy. Like a cup of hot chocolate after being out in the snow. That's what love had always seemed like to her.

What she felt when she was with T'arq was so far from

that it wasn't funny. It was scorching, incendiary... it felt as if she would die if he didn't touch her.

She pulled the pillow away and threw it across the room.

Was it time to let love go? It wasn't as if she would find it with T'arq. That was obvious enough. He was notorious for sleeping around. One night and then move on. But oh, what a night. She tried, but couldn't find it in herself to regret it.

But a little piece of her wondered if it had meant anything more to him. He had seemed almost shaken, reverent. He was not what she had expected.

She rubbed her temples.

What did it all mean?

Krystal sighed and pulled the sheet up from where it had become tangled around her feet. Did it matter? He had left without saying goodbye, sneaking out before she woke up and had to speak with her. And they had to work with each other, at least until this cloak was tested and then rolled out across the fleet. It would make it harder to work with him for the next few weeks, sure, but she could manage. She would have to manage.

Dragging herself from the bed, Krystal made her way into the shower and was, not for the first time, thankful that the hot water was instantaneous and plentiful. She soaped her hair and ran her hands over her body, wincing as she touched tender places. She had finger marks on her hips, she realized, spreading her hand to match the print, her hand so much smaller. And was that a hickey on her neck?

Oh great. That was going to be fun to cover up. At least she had material for her wank bank for the rest of her life. Because she didn't think anyone would ever live up to that.

She pushed thoughts of T'arq and his wicked tongue out

of her mind. She quickly finished washing and was wrapping a towel around herself when the buzzer for her door sounded.

Her heart thumped rapidly as she rushed to the door, which slid open with a gush of cool air from the corridor to reveal... not T'arq, but Laila.

Oh.

A dull ache settled in her chest. Had she really thought that he had come back for her? Yes, she had. She spun away, hiding her face.

"What happened in here?" Laila stood just inside the doorway and looked around the small room, eyes wide.

It was a bit of a mess. More so than usual. The sheet had come loose from the bottom of the mattress, the blankets in a heap at the foot of the bed. Clothes were strewn haphazardly around the room, draped over the armchair and across the floor.

Krystal hid a smile behind her hand, pretending to stifle a yawn. "Nothing."

"Nothing? Really?"

"Yes?"

Laila crossed her arms. "You're my little sister, Krystal. I thought I told you to stay away from him."

Krystal stomped toward the wardrobe that was built into the wall near the bed and retrieved a clean uniform and underwear. Disappearing into the bathroom, she slid the door shut.

"You can't just run away from this, Krys!" Laila shouted through the door.

Krystal didn't bother to reply, fighting to control her

temper. She quickly dressed and squeezed the water from her hair with the towel, opting to leave it loose to dry.

Opening the door, she confronted her sister, who was bending to pick something up from the floor. "What is this?" She held up a sock. A very large sock. One that belonged to an equally large warrior that had been warming her bed only hours before.

"It's a sock, Laila."

"I can see that. What's it doing here?"

"Minding its own business, I would imagine." She pushed a pile of clothes from the armchair onto the floor to sit and pull on her socks and boots. Adding, under her breath, "like I wish you would."

"I just don't want you to get hurt."

That was it. It was bad enough that everyone else on this ship treated her like a child, but her own sister?

She stood and turned to face Laila, hands on her hips. "I'm short, not five years old. What exactly do you want to protect me from?"

Laila gaped, mouth opening and closing like a fish gasping for air.

"I'm not a child!" Krystal shook her finger at her sister. "What I choose to do with my life is my business." She crossed her arms and cocked her hip, sending Laila a glare for good measure. "If I want to have sex with a hot as fuck alien dude with a donkey cock, then I will. OK?"

Laila's hid her mouth behind a hand, her eyes crinkling at the corners.

"Don't you dare laugh."

She snorted, her eyes dancing. Finally, gathering enough breath to speak, she choked out. "Donkey cock?"

Krystal's lips twitched. "I don't kiss and tell."

Laila laughed, wiping tears from her eyes before sobering. "I'm sorry, Krys. With mom and dad gone..."

Krystal's anger dissolved, and she cleared the few paces between them to wrap her arms around her sister in a hug. "I know it's your way of showing you love me."

"Hey! I remember you asking if Zac had two dicks." Laila gave her a pointed look.

Krystal giggled. "I did, didn't I?"

They shared a smile and stood, side by side, surveilling the carnage. "Well, at least you two had a good time."

Krystal snorted and smacked Laila lightly on the arm. "No comment."

———

The hangar was busy with small hover transporters running gear to and from stealth ships and shuttles. Krystal dodged a bot that almost crashed into her feet, making a mental note to ask about increasing the collision avoidance buffer.

Spying Laila and Zac, she broke into a jog as she crossed the hangar to the small shuttle where they were standing.

"How's the cloak?"

"Good. I'll need to check a few things, but I think I fixed it."

Zac smiled a rare smile. "That's great news. We'll need every advantage we can get for this next mission."

"Oh?" Krystal knew better than to ask for details of Zac and Laila's missions, even if she was now privy to what their team actually did.

Zac's answer was lost as a familiar figure appeared from the far side of the shuttle behind the lowered ramp, a wicked grin on his face.

Oh boy. Hold it together, Krystal.

T'arq sauntered up to her slowly, stopping within touching distance to grab a latch on the undercarriage of the shuttle above his head and stretch his arms. He was huge like that, able to reach over nine feet off the ground. Krystal's eyes were glued to where his hands flexed around the latch, his hands that had worked her into a blubbering mess last night, flexing and sending the muscles in his forearms rolling. The sleeves of his flight suit had been pulled down and tied around his waist in a knot, his chest barely contained by a black tee that strained against the defined muscles.

She swallowed, wondering if it was possible to choke on your own tongue while you were conscious.

"Don't you mean I fixed it?" His eyes flashed dark purple as he winked at her.

"What?" She gave him a blank look.

"The cloak. You said I was a genius, remember?" He grinned.

She rolled her eyes, finally dragging them away from him and focusing over his left shoulder. "You just reminded me of something, that's all."

That's the best he can do?

Her chest squeezed, and she swallowed past the hurt. It was probably a good thing she hadn't asked him how he felt about her last night. It seemed pretty obvious that he hadn't changed. A one night kind of guy, and then pretend everything was fine the next day? She blinked hard.

Don't cry. Not here. Not now. Not where he can see.

"Hmm, and what do I remind you of?"

Krystal felt the blush flood her face. Shit. She shot a glance at Laila, who was watching them with narrowed eyes.

"Yes, Krystal. What did he remind you of?" Laila lifted an eyebrow, which Krystal ignored.

"He said it was predictable what the Xakul would do."

T'arq dropped his hands. "What's that got to do with the cloak?"

Krystal nodded to herself. It had seemed all too simple when she had figured it out. "The algorithm was too predictable. It was projecting a cloaked image, but it wasn't irregular."

Talk about work. I can do that.

"Why would that be a problem?" Laila asked.

Krystal fiddled with the sleeve of her uniform. "Do you remember that old movie with the sandworms?"

"Dune?" Laila's face lit up. It was one of her favorite movies.

"That's the one! Why do they walk that weird way over the sands?"

Laila nodded. "Because they don't want to attract the worm."

"Exactly."

"So the cloak needs to be less predictable to not attract the Xakul's attention?" Laila mused.

Krystal nodded.

"Pre-flight checks all clear?" Zac asked T'arq, drawing Krystal's attention away from her sister.

"All clear. We are good to go."

"We're just waiting on Domik and CJ, and then we'll get going."

Zac and Laila shouldered packs of gear and headed up the ramp and into the cargo hold of the shuttle, leaving T'arq and Krystal alone. Krystal took a step to one side to get around T'arq and onto the ramp, but he mimicked her, blocking her path.

"I've decided you aren't a little mouse," T'arq's voice was like water, rolling over her. Completely different to how he spoke to anyone else, she mused in a distant part of her brain that was still functioning.

"Hello!" She jerked as if scalded, turning to see CJ jog toward them, the blonde medic carrying a large satchel with a red cross on it. "I didn't know you were joining us, Krystal."

"She's not," T'arq replied.

"Yes, she is." Domik dropped that bomb as he strode past the small group and into the hold of the shuttle, CJ following him up the ramp.

"Krys?" T'arq swung to address her, hands on his hips. "You said nothing."

Krystal scoffed. It wasn't as if they had talked much. It wasn't as if she meant anything to him for him to be concerned for her. Right?

"You need me for this mission. What if something goes wrong with the cloak? How are you going to fix it?"

T'arq reached out, touching her shoulder as his eyes lightened to pale lilac. So light they almost disappeared into the whites of his eyes. "I want nothing to happen to you."

"Well, isn't that the theme of the day?" she muttered, looking at the ground and taking a deep breath. She pushed her shoulders back and tossed her head. "I am an adult and, yes, I have some issues being in space, but this shuttle is bigger—"

"Not by much." He dropped his hand, grumbling.

"—and I can do this." She refused to let him talk over her, taking a step to the side once more and, this time, making it around him and onto the cargo ramp.

"It's not that I don't think you can—"

"Then why? What am I to you?" She glared down at him from her elevated position on the ramp.

He didn't answer, just stared up at her, lips pressed together in a thin line.

Laila appeared at the top of the ramp and cleared her throat. "Are you two done?"

Krystal turned away from T'arq and marched into the cargo hold. "Quite done, I think."

CHAPTER NINETEEN

T'arq

T'arq growled and punched the side of the shuttle, groaning when his hand throbbed. He cradled it against his chest and sighed. He was terrified that she would be hurt, but he was also so proud of her and what she had overcome. It wasn't a matter of whether she could do it—he knew she could—it was that he didn't want anything to happen to her.

Especially not after last night.

Last night had been a miscalculation. How could he possibly have thought he could go to see her and just talk? He scoffed. As soon as he'd seen her with that blanket wrapped around her, he had wanted to carry her off somewhere and keep her safe.

What was wrong with him?

"What? Did you think punching a ship would feel pleasant?" Zac's amused voice broke into his turbid thoughts.

T'arq glared at his friend and commander. "Does she have to come?"

Zac leaned against the side of the cargo hold doorway, arms crossed. "Is that what's bothering you?"

"I don't want her to get hurt."

"So keep her safe."

T'arq barked a humorless laugh. "Tried that already, ended up spacing her." Sending Krystal into space on her own was the hardest thing he had ever done. He never wanted to feel like that again. He had been so certain he would die, but he'd been prepared to so long as she survived.

He had been ready to sacrifice himself for her.

And when they had both survived? What had he done? He'd lied to her. It didn't matter that he had no choice; it wasn't as if he could tell her he was part of a covert squad that completed missions that nobody wanted to ever be made public. He had still lied.

She didn't trust him and that hurt. And, in the early hours of the morning as he watched her sleep, it was that realization that had sent him running from her room like a coward.

"We have work to do and she's coming on the mission, whether you like it or not. Let's go." Zac's tone broached no argument, and T'arq knew better than to try, so he stalked up the ramp and into the spacious cargo hold.

Thankfully, this shuttle was much bigger than the stealth ship. The cargo hold was small, and currently empty, as their mission was a short one and they weren't transporting anything. There were rings and straps to tie bulky items down, which were currently stowed behind cargo nets, the elastic mesh stretching the length of the hold and from floor to ceiling.

The cargo hold was separated from the rest of the ship by a wall, split only by a narrow corridor that ran the length of the ship to show a glimpse of the cockpit. There was a tiny multi-purpose space between the cargo hold and the cockpit, which was currently configured with bench seating on one side where Domik was lounging, his hands behind his head and eyes closed. On the other side, CJ was stowing her pack in a locker with her name on it.

T'arq nodded in greeting as he passed into the cockpit. The ramp into the cargo hold was one of two entrances. The second was a door into the cockpit that could be accessed by a short flight of retractable steps. There were two seats at the very front of the ship, one for the pilot the other for the co-pilot. Krystal was already seated in the co-pilot's chair and turned around in her seat to watch him approach. There was more seating around the outside of the space—pull-down seats that were not comfortable during long trips—where Zac and Laila were adjusting their harnesses.

It was a small battleship; the hull reinforced to prevent the penetrative rounds the Xakul liked to use in addition to their own plasma weapons. Which was what they needed, as they were about to go into battle.

"Everyone here?" T'arq asked as he slid into the pilot's chair next to Krystal.

As Zac answered T'arq in the affirmative, Krystal turned to watch him strap himself into the seat.

"Are you going to be OK?" he asked. "The last time..." This was a bad idea. She really shouldn't be here.

"I'll be fine," she replied, tucking her hair behind her ear and smoothing her hands over her flight suit. She picked up the tablet in front of her and began tapping the screen.

"You don't need to do this, Krystal."

Her brown eyes were serious as they lifted to meet his. "Neither do you."

"This is my job. It's what I do."

"And this," she gestured with the tablet at the shuttle, "is what I do."

He sighed and looked away, hands moving automatically to finish the pre-flight checks. This model of shuttle was what he had flown when he had first earned his commission. He had spent years ferrying troops in and out of battles with the Xakul, so often that he could find his way around the controls in the dark. Which he had actually had to do more than once.

If she would not stay behind, then he needed to do everything in his power to keep her safe... or at least as safe as possible, considering the circumstances.

"Krystal—"

A siren filled the cabin. A quick check of the display showed exactly what he didn't want to see.

"Fuck." That came from the usually stoic Zac.

Krystal turned to look at T'arq. "What is that?" A tremor made her voice waver.

"Xakul," T'arq said darkly, watching out of the large view screen as Taurean ground troops scurried about on the floor of the hangar.

"Domik! CJ! Strap in. We're heading out!" Zac shouted, head turned toward the rear of the shuttle.

The siren continued to wail in the background, the sound grating as T'arq began powering up the engines. Domik and CJ hurried into the cockpit, taking their seats and strapping in. That was everyone, then. T'arq's hands moved fluidly over the controls, shutting the cargo hold door and performing the last checks before they would leave. The shuttle vibrated as they prepared for takeoff.

The shipboard comm broadcasted into the cockpit. "Zataras to all combat ships. We have confirmed contact with Xakul fighters."

"They're attacking the Zataras?" Krystal asked, eyes wide.

The lights in the hangar flickered, then went out as the shuttle shook.

"Get us out of here, T'arq!" Zac ordered.

"Working on it." The shuttle lifted and hovered about the hangar floor before turning to face the hangar bay entrance. "Shit. The hangar doors are shut."

"Give me a second and I'll see if I can get them open." Krystal's fingers flew over her tablet. "I've connected to the Zataras and the doors are... cycling after the power outage. I'll just try... there!" She threw her hands in the air with a triumphant shout, the hangar doors opening.

"Nicely done, specialist." T'arq grinned and powered the shuttle forward and toward the slowly opening shuttle bay doors.

"Are we going to fit?"

T'arq threw his head back and laughed.

Krystal yelped as he spun the shuttle, and it slipped through the gap and out into space. "That was close."

"You haven't seen anything yet, little mouse."

They shot into the space around the Zataras along with stealth ships and other craft. One by one, they winked out of sight as their pilots engaged the cloaks.

"It's working!" Krystal's excited shout brought a smile to

T'arq's face, but he dared not break his concentration to look at her. The Xakul were getting too close for comfort.

Tomas' voice filled the cabin as the comm opened with the Zataras. "Zac, I need you to hit their base. You will have to do it alone. I can't afford to let any other ships go while we're under attack."

"Yes, sir," Zac replied, then after the comm signal with the Zataras had closed he addressed the crew of the small shuttle. "Right, team. We have been tasked with destroying the Xakul base that T'arq and Krystal found. This is our best chance while so many of their fighters are engaged here. This will not be a simple assignment, but if anyone can do it, we can."

A series of battle cries came from the crew.

T'arq watched as first a handful of Xakul fighters appeared on the display, then more and more until they formed a massive swarm. This was beyond anything he had ever seen in all his years as a warrior. Taurean ships formed defensive positions around the Zataras, darting in seemingly incomprehensible patterns. Small stealth ships darted around larger shuttles, protecting them from Xakul attack. The shuttles couldn't move as quickly as the stealth ships, but what they lacked in that department they more than made up for in fire power.

T'arq watched as one Xakul ship darted forward as it fired at one of the larger shuttles, the stealth ships protecting it, dancing away to open a corridor to the enemy ship. The plasma charge from the shuttle was fast and almost blinding in its intensity, and in a flash the Xakul shuttle exploded, quickly burning up in the vacuum of space. The stealth ships slid back into position, ready for the next round.

"Krystal? Is our cloak ready?" T'arq dodged around a group of Taurean fighters that were in hot pursuit of a Xakul fighter.

"Yes." Her reply was steady, her movements sure as she tapped rapidly on the screen.

"Now would be the perfect time to use it!" His hands flew over the controls, sending the ship into a dive to avoid an exploding Taurean ship.

"Was that—"

"Now!" He gritted his teeth, using all his skill to maneuver the shuttle away from the Zataras, dodging between space battles until, a few nail-biting minutes later, they had cleared the fracas and were heading for the asteroid field.

Relieved laughter came from the seats behind T'arq. "Domik, for a big dude, you can really dance!" CJ laughed.

"That makes no sense, woman." The giant Taurean unfurled himself from the seat and headed back to the galley.

"Sure it does," she said, following him. Their voices disappearing to a background hum.

T'arq chuckled.

"What's with those two?" Krystal inclined her head at the retreating pair.

"Who? Domik and CJ?" T'arq looked at her in surprise. "Nothing."

"I wouldn't be so sure about that."

Checking to make sure there were no Xakul ships following them, T'arq turned in his seat to watch Krystal. She had made it through a space battle without batting an eyelid. Well, almost.

"You did well, little mouse."

"I did, didn't I?" she said, sitting up a little straighter. "Better than last time, right?"

"Are you kidding me? Last time you barely made it out of the hangar. This time you were in a proper battle."

Krystal stared at the viewscreen, watching the asteroid field grow larger as they approached. "Maybe I just needed exposure therapy or something." One side of her mouth lifted in an amused smirk.

"Or maybe it's the company?"

She gave him a thoughtful look but didn't answer, instead turning back to look out the window.

Domik emerged from the galley, CJ trailing him with a steaming cup of coffee in her hands. She blew on it and took a sip before speaking. "So, what's the plan when we reach the baddies?"

Domik rolled his eyes, a movement that T'arq would have missed—and never believed had happened—except he'd turned around at CJ's question.

Laila answered, "We bomb the fuck out of them."

"We have a problem," Zac said. "Incoming Xakul fighters!"

CHAPTER TWENTY

Krystal

Stiffening at Zac's proclamation, Krystal checked the viewscreen. "Nine fighters... no ten," she said, her fingers racing across the controls. She turned her head to look at T'arq. "They're on an intercept course."

"I see them. Are you ready?"

She nodded.

"Do you trust me?"

She glanced at him, surprised to see he looked nervous as he bit his bottom lip and fidgeted. And then she realized she didn't need to think about it. She did trust him. More than she trusted anyone. T'arq would not hurt her. He would do nothing to cause her pain. And if he asked if she would jump out of an airlock, well, hadn't she already done that?

"Yes." She smiled gently.

He grinned in return and reached across to cup her face in one hand. Maybe she meant something to him after all?

Still watching her, he turned his head to call over his shoulder. "Zac? How about we play dead?"

A laugh that met T'arq's question. "Sure."

"Play dead?" Krystal asked quietly.

"Turn the cloak off."

"What?" The cloak was the only thing keeping them from being seen. She stiffened in her seat.

"Do you trust me?" He repeated.

Hadn't she just said that she did? Grumbling to herself about stupid men and their risk-taking behavior, she turned the cloak off, feeling a sick feeling in her stomach at how exposed they were.

T'arq flicked a switch, and a pre-recorded distress message was broadcast from the shuttle.

"We'll get them closer and then surprise them." T'arq grinned. "Works every time." He powered down the main engines, leaving only the stabilizing thrusters that were used for ship to ship docking. "Here," he said, gesturing to the power button for the thrusters, "just push that randomly every few seconds. Try to make it look like we're struggling to get the engines going."

"But don't they get used to it?" She pushed the button and felt the ship jerk slightly as the thrusters engaged and stop when she lifted her finger from the button.

"You'd think, but they don't. We're not sure why."

"They've taken the bait," Domik said.

Krystal engaged the thrusters again, this time only on one side of the shuttle, so they spun slightly, and then the opposite side to have them spin back again.

"Nice." T'arq grinned at her.

The Xakul ship approached slowly, circling their shuttle

at a safe distance. Light danced over the dark hull of the ship, like the exoskeleton of the Xakul soldiers. As the ship moved, the colors changed, rippling along the side of the ship like oil on water.

What material did they use in their ships? No material that Krystal knew would behave in such a way.

"Plasma cannon or grenade?" Domik asked.

"Plasma cannon. Let's make sure they won't follow us," Zac replied.

Domik swiftly primed the cannon and trained the sights on the ship that was unwittingly making its way into the trap.

Krystal waited; breath held. Her heart beat so fast she pressed a hand to her sternum. This was far too similar to what had happened with T'arq.

She didn't realize she was almost hyperventilating until T'arq reached across and took her chin in his hand to turn her face to meet his. His eyes were so beautiful. How come she hadn't realized that they had a dark blue rim around the outside?

"Breathe, Krys." His deep voice was slow and calming, and she took deep, steady breaths.

She nodded her thanks and offered a small smile. She could do this. She would do this. Krystal hit the thrusters once more, sending the ship into a slight roll.

"They're getting within range."

"Wait, Domik. I want them closer." Zac was focused on the Xakul ship which suddenly turned to face them head on. "Fire!"

With a flick of his wrist, Domik struck the enemy ship with a blast from the plasma cannon. The hull was torn in two, an explosion sending debris spiraling away from where the Xakul ship had been moments before.

T'arq quickly powered up their vessel. "Cloak up."

Krystal engaged the cloak once more and T'arq flew the ship away from the wreckage of their vanquished foe.

"Nice work, Domik." T'arq turned to grin at the usually stoic weapons specialist, whose mouth tilted in reply.

Their original trip into the asteroid field had felt like a long voyage, because she had spent so much time collecting data and T'arq had taken an indirect flight path. But this time they flew directly toward their target, and Krystal realized just how close the Zataras was to the Xakul stronghold. She pulled up the navigation screen and, checking their location, estimated that it would take them less than a quarter of the time to arrive, even if the shuttle they were using was much slower than the stealth ship.

They moved into the asteroid belt, hiding occasionally to avoid passing Xakul ships, though they were few. Were most of them engaged in the battle with the Zataras? She shuddered, wondering how the big starship was faring in the attack, but then pushed the thought away to focus on the task in front of her.

Krystal glanced at T'arq sitting next to her.

"Ready?" he asked.

"Yes," she replied, surprised to find that it was the truth.

As one, they flew the shuttle to where they had seen the Xakul's fake asteroid base. Krystal was surprised to see it wasn't as big as she remembered, although it was much larger than the Zataras. It was just a big rock.

"Comms are down," CJ reported with a nervous laugh.

"That signal jammer must be still going," T'arq said, tapping his fingers on the arm of his chair.

A door on the side of the rock slid back and a Xakul fighter emerged, flying directly toward them.

"Have they seen us?" She whispered.

"Can they?" T'arq replied.

"I don't think so." She knew the Xakul should not be able to see them, but there was still a part of her that was nervous about being found.

An eerie quiet descended on the cockpit as they watched the Xakul fighter approach them. Closer and closer it drew, and Krystal's heart pounded faster and faster. The ship flew so close to them they could see the Xakul pilot in the cockpit. Krystal shuddered as it passed over them, releasing a breath she didn't realize she had been holding.

"Feel better now?" T'arq asked, patting her hand.

"Yes," she took a few deep breaths, forcing her heart rate to calm, "but I'll be a lot better when we're back on the starship...assuming it is still in one piece."

"I know the feeling," he muttered, his lips pressed together in a grim line.

"Domik, get those charges ready," Zac ordered. "T'arq and Krystal, keep the cloak up and be ready to move any moment. CJ, keep checking the comms. I don't like being this isolated from the Zataras."

Domik was part of the way through priming the explosive charges when an alert popped up on Krystal's screen.

"I think we have company," she said, pointing to where a series of dots had appeared. She zoomed in to see a swarm of Xakul ships approaching their position.

"Shit."

CHAPTER TWENTY-ONE

T'arq

Just what they needed right now. T'arq cursed as he moved the shuttle into a defensive position, angled to make best use of the heavy guns manned by Domik.

They were meant to get in and out quickly; blow up the Xakul base and get back to the Zataras. They did not have time, or the firepower, to get into a battle with a fleet of Xakul fighters. T'arq was a superb pilot, but he knew the extent of his abilities, and trying to outgun an entire fleet of the enemy? Definitely not something he would do.

Especially not with Krystal on board.

She had improved significantly since their last trip, but she was still nervous. T'arq wasn't sure that anyone else could tell, but she was jiggling her knee up and down as she worked and humming under her breath quietly.

She always hummed when she was nervous.

"We have one chance to get this right," Zac said. "And we

are not going home without destroying that base. I don't need to remind you all of what's at stake."

Murmured agreements came from the crew as Zac looked around at everyone.

"How much longer on the charges, Domik?"

"Done."

"Good. T'arq, get us to the first location and make it quick."

"On it," he replied, the shuttle shooting from where he had hidden them, tucked away under an overhand on a large asteroid. Now they were heading into the open. He felt eerily exposed, like he'd walked out in public with no clothes on.

"Do you trust this cloak?" Zac asked T'arq.

T'arq looked from his friend and commander to Krystal, her worried face making his chest tighten. "I do." He smiled reassuringly, and Krystal's lips turned upwards ever so slightly, as if she was trying to put on a brave face.

It was in that moment that he realized that he never wanted to let her go. His eyes widened and his breath caught.

"What's wrong?" Krystal asked, reaching out a hand to touch his arm.

He looked down at her fingers, so small on his arm, and back up at her. "Nothing. Everything is perfect."

Her face scrunched up as she spoke. "Are you kidding me? We're all alone, away from the Zataras, about to blow up a Xakul base, with no backup and," she stopped pulling her hand back and spluttering as if trying to find the words, "the Zataras itself was being attacked by the same bugs who actually eat people, so who knows if it will even exist when we try to go back."

T'arq nodded. All of that was correct. He couldn't argue

with her. "That's true."

She continued, "And you think this is perfect?" Her voice had risen in volume as she spoke, her eyebrows shot up and she squeaked the last few words.

Despite the considerable issues in their situation, T'arq was calm. He didn't reply, just smiled, taking in her flushed face and bright eyes.

"You're insane." She turned away with a dismissive wave of her hand.

"You said we." He reached out and placed her hand back on his arm, his fingers on the back of her hand making soothing strokes over her skin.

That's better.

"What?" She glanced up from where she was watching his hand on hers.

"You said we're all alone, but we're not. We're together. So everything is perfect." He turned away to focus on bringing the shuttle to the first location where they would lay their charges, releasing her arm.

He pretended not to notice as Krystal's mouth dropped open, blinking at him in surprise.

"Let's get in close then and cause some chaos!" Laila called out.

CJ let out a whoop, shouting, "Let's kick some ass!"

T'arq turned around in time to see Domik barely lift an eyebrow at the enthusiastic medic, before grumbling something under his breath.

CJ turned around and poked him in the back with her finger. "Just you wait, big guy. I'll get you on your knees."

Domik stiffened, but CJ had already whirled away to slide back into the seat at her station, where she donned her headset. T'arq lifted an eyebrow at Domik, who ignored him, turning back to his station.

"Ready?" he asked Krystal, who nodded jerkily.

The Xakul stronghold loomed in front of them, T'arq slowing the shuttle as they neared. They had approached out of the immediate sight of the hangar bay that Krystal and T'arq had seen the first time. Zac hadn't wanted to take any chances with being seen, and T'arq was happy to oblige him.

"Almost at the first location," T'arq said.

Working seamlessly, Domik loaded the explosive charges and, when the ship was in place, guided them remotely into place on the outside of the Xakul base.

"How do they work?" Krystal asked.

"Domik's the weapons specialist." CJ nodded toward the big Taurean, who turned at his name.

"The charge is on a timer. When we're safely out of the way, we'll detonate them. They stick to any surface with a dynamic bond. It's pretty simple," Domik said.

"That has to be the most you've said in one go since I've met you," CJ called with a laugh.

T'arq looked up in time to see Domik roll his eyes, the human expression so unexpected that T'arq gaped.

"What?" Domik scowled.

"Nothing."

They moved as quickly as they could, the pressing need to get done and get out of there settling a grim silence over the bridge. They had just placed the last charge and were moving away when an alarm sounded.

"What's that?" Laila asked, pointing at the viewscreen where a sinister-looking dark shape was stalking across the outside of the enemy base.

"I don't know," Zac said, leaning forward and zooming in to enlarge the view.

A collective gasp was heard as they realized what they were looking at. A blocky shape with four legs moved across the rocky surface of the base as it approached the place where the charge had been laid. It was huge, easily the height of two Taureans. Its exterior was the same dark material that shone with a technicolor riot that flowed across what had to be a cabin to house a Xakul operator. The four legs moved in a strange dance, not forward and backwards, but as if the legs could move any way it desired. It stopped and a robotic arm extended.

"Is that...?" Krystal whispered.

"Some kind of robotic tank? Yeah, looks like it." T'arq's mouth pressed into a line as he moved their shuttle further away.

"What's it doing?" Krystal asked.

"Getting blown up," Domik replied, as the robotic arm on the Xakul tank pulled at the explosive charge. T'arq didn't wait for an instruction, but flew the shuttle away from the Xakul base as quickly as he could.

"Shit," CJ said. "There are more of those things, and they've found the charges."

"How many of the charges?" Zac asked.

"All of them."

Well, that wasn't good. It was one thing to do missions like this when it was just him, when he didn't care about anyone else. But now? He glanced at Krystal, his stomach twisting as he bit his lip.

"Are we far enough away, Domik?" Zac asked.

"We're still in the blast radius, but..." he tapped on the

screen, face scrunched up as he concentrated, "... we'll take significant damage."

"Too late," T'arq muttered as the first of the blasts came, the shock wave making the shuttle shake.

"Everyone strap in! This is going to be rough." T'arq called as debris rocketed past them, chunks of metal and rock striking the shuttle, each causing him to wince.

"Did all the charges go?" Krystal asked, her hands twisting together as she bit her lip.

"No, that was just one," T'arq replied grimly.

"Remind me how many charges we put out?" she choked out.

"Twenty-six."

"Fuck." She closed her eyes and gripped the handsets of the co-pilot's chair.

T'arq couldn't agree more. If they didn't get away, they were going to be blown to bits with the rest of the enemy base, caught up in the blast wave that would rip them into pieces. He pushed the shuttle to move as fast as it could away from the Xakul position.

A second blast was chased by a third until there was a cascade of explosions that rocked the ship repeatedly. T'arq flew like he had never flown before, using everything at his disposal to dodge flying pieces of debris and rock as they shot through the asteroid belt at a pace he would have previously considered reckless.

A siren sounded.

"Incoming Xakul fighters," Laila said.

"Domik?" Zac asked.

"Plasma cannon primed and ready," he replied.

Zac scanned a tablet in his hand before tapping the

screen decisively with a finger. "T'arq, can you take us on a route that will weave through all those fighters? Let's finish the job."

T'arq grinned. "I thought you'd never ask." This was the flying he lived for. "Ready for a wild ride?"

"You mean that wasn't wild?" She gaped.

"Now, T'arq!" Zac shouted.

T'arq had no time to reply as he flew the shuttle into the middle of the closest group of Xakul. As soon as they were within range, Domik blasted the lead ship with the plasma cannon. T'arq dodged and weaved between fighters, over the top, and underneath, before sailing easily through the gap and away from the enemy fleet, which now resembled a heap of space junk.

As he plotted the route out of the asteroid field, he glanced at Krystal, who was gripping the armrests tightly, her face pale. "Are you ok, Krys?"

"Have you ever been on a rollercoaster?" She choked out.

He had no idea what she was talking about it. "What?"

"Never mind. Yes, I'm fine. Never better. Totally wonderful. Absolutely amazing." Her words were punctuated by the bouncing of one knee.

T'arq grinned. She was nervous, but he knew exactly what to do. He sang. A burst of laughter came from behind him and soon Laila had joined in, and then CJ and finally Krystal.

And that's how T'arq came to be flying a cloaked shuttle away from Xakul fighters while singing Highway to the Danger Zone.

A s the Zataras emerged in their sights, T'arq was thankful to see no Xakul in sight. Or at least, none that weren't now space junk.

"Ooo. Someone had a bad day," CJ joked, and Tarq's lips twitched in amusement.

He guided the ship into the hangar, setting the shuttle down in its designated spot and powering down the engines. As the ship's pressure equalized with that of the starship, T'arq opened the ramp to the cargo hold so the crew could disembark.

The hangar bay was filled with Taureans and humans alike. Repair crews were working on damaged ships while those that were ready to be flown were being refueled. People rushed this way and that, the overall effect chaotic.

T'arq stepped off the ramp, the last to leave the shuttle. Krystal was standing with Laila, heads close together as they talked. His chest felt tight as he took a step closer. She glanced at him, then turned and walked away.

"Krystal?" He called out, but she didn't turn. He called again, louder, "Krystal!"

She stopped, and squaring her shoulders, turned to face him. "Yes?"

He stalked toward her, stopping when he was just outside of arm's reach. He didn't trust himself to just reach out and pull her into his arms. This was important. He couldn't screw this up.

"Can we talk?" He rubbed his hands on his flight suit.

He had never been this nervous before. Not when facing down hordes of Xakul. Not when he had started at the Taurean military academy as a boy where he knew nobody.

"About what?" She looked up at him, brown curls loose around her shoulders, and his breath caught. He had known beautiful women before, some would say countless beautiful women and, though T'arq knew that was untrue, he did nothing to dispel the rumors. But with Krystal? He wanted her to see him for who he was and not what people thought he was.

He shifted from foot to foot and looked around at the curious faces that had stopped to watch. This was not a conversation he wanted to have in public. "Can we talk... in private?"

She raised an eyebrow. "T'arq, the last time you came to talk to me in private, we didn't get any talking done."

He ignored CJ's giggle.

"Krystal—"

"Come on, T'arq. Out with it!" Zac smirked, lifting an eyebrow at T'arq's glare.

After the way T'arq had needled Zac over Laila, he should have expected it, but that didn't mean he couldn't scowl at his friend. A friend who laughed outright at his put-out expression.

T'arq turned to face Krystal, ignoring everyone and everything around them. His world narrowed to just the two of them as he took a step closer to her. She was delicate, but strong. Fierce. He needed to tell her how he felt. But he would not do so in front of everyone. She wouldn't like that.

"Trust me?" he asked, her answer more important to him than air.

His chest loosened as she nodded and placed her hand in his.

CHAPTER TWENTY-TWO

Krystal

His strong but gentle grip on her hand warmed her from inside, and she smiled up at him, squeezing his fingers.

"I trust you, T'arq."

He turned and led her from the hangar, her shorter steps making her trot after him. When they had passed out of sight of the busy scene, T'arq stopped, Krystal plowing into the back of him at the unexpected change. He swung her up into his arms, muttering something about being impatient and needing to get her alone. One brawny arm gripped under her thighs, the other around her shoulders. She snuggled into the warm strength of him.

Be still, my frantically beating heart.

As he walked, she breathed in his scent. The familiar spice of his skin was intoxicating, and she closed her eyes, letting her head rest against his chest. Her fingers wandered over his shoulders and neck, trailing patterns against his skin.

He stiffened when she brushed against a particularly sensitive place, a low growl coming from deep in his chest.

"Too much?" she asked.

"Never."

His answer sent a shiver through her.

Krystal let his smooth steps rock her into a contented doze, not paying attention to where they were going until a door opened and T'arq placed her gently down on her feet.

She pulled away to turn and look around. "These are your quarters?"

He nodded and stood near the door as she looked around.

They were much larger, and much neater, than hers. There was a couch instead of an armchair, and the bed was huge. There was a counter along one wall with built-in cupboards, which she knew would house the food replication unit. Its basic style was very much like her own quarters, but he had decorated it differently. There was a purple throw over the couch, and a rug that looked like it had been handwoven hanging on the wall above the bed. The bedspread was in various shades of purple as well, as were the throw cushions that were piled up against the headboard.

"What do you think?" he asked.

"It's not what I expected," she admitted, one brow quirked in question. "Why the purple?"

He shrugged. "It's your favorite color."

She whirled to face him, gesturing at the decor. "You did this for me? When?"

He rubbed the back of his neck and looked at the floor, muttering. "After Zac and Laila's wedding."

She strolled toward the couch, picking up a cushion and

stroking the velvety fabric absently. "But that was months ago."

"I know." He scuffed his foot on the carpet.

"And we met at their wedding." She hugged the cushion to her chest, as if it would act like a shield against the revelation of his feelings for her.

He paused, biting his lip. His answer was simple, when eventually it came. "Yes."

She sat heavily on the couch; the cushion still clutched tightly in her hands. "You mean you decorated like this after having only met me once? And you did it because my favorite color is purple?"

He kneeled in front of her. "Yes, Krystal. You were wearing a green dress, and I commented on the color. You said that green was nice, but purple was your favorite."

She nodded slowly. "Yes, I remember that dress. But I still don't understand."

He sat back on his haunches in front of her, at the same eye level as her. "I know you've been warned against me. I won't defend myself against the things people have said because I don't care what people think. I never have. Except for you. I care very much what you think about me." He gestured around the room with a hand. "I would do anything for you."

She blinked; her expression unreadable. Not the reaction he had hoped for.

"Krystal, please say something."

Krystal stared at him for long, silent moments, eyes wide. She had to be dreaming. There was no way that he had felt like this about her for that long. No way. It just wasn't possible. She must have hit her head on the shuttle and be knocked out cold. There was no other explanation.

If this is a dream, then there's only one thing for it.

Krystal launched herself at him, sending him flying backwards to land on the floor on his back with her straddling his hips. She braced her hands on his shoulders and leaned forward, her hair creating a curtain around them, stopping with her face so close to his they were touching noses.

"Do you mean it?"

His eyes narrowed at her. "I never say things I don't mean, Krystal. But if I have to convince you, I will." He lifted his head to capture her lips with his, sliding one of his hands up to cup her ass and drag her against him, the other sliding up her back to pull her down against him. He broke away, breathing hard, eyes a deep purple, and the pupils blown out. "I will worship you until you believe me." He grinned and lifted his head to nip her bottom lip with his teeth.

She moaned as he released her. "All right."

His eyebrows drew together in confusion, and she lifted a hand to smooth them. "Sorry?"

"All right... I'll let you worship me." She giggled as he rolled her over onto her back.

"You are no little mouse. You're a cat," he stood and lifted her to her feet. "My little cat." He pressed the zipper of her flight suit down, exposing her bra and the curve of her stomach before brushing his knuckles over her panties. "Like your underwear." He lifted an eyebrow as his lips twitched at the sight of the cartoon animals.

Her heart beat like a fluttering bird. "Don't you mean kitten?"

He slid her arms free, dropping a kiss to the curve where her neck met her shoulder, the suit sliding down her skin like a caress to pool at her hips. He dropped to his knees in front of her and tugged at the fabric, helping her off with her boots and to step free.

"Kitten?" he asked.

"A baby feline, remember?"

"Oh, you are far too wild to be a baby anything." He stood and quickly stripped himself of his own clothes before he was standing naked in front of her.

"Nobody has ever called me wild."

His eyes were fiery as they traveled over her exposed skin. "Then they didn't know you."

Oh.

Her eyes slid over him, all golden skin over heavy muscles and that thick cock that was straining like a divining rod toward her. She took a step closer and reached for him, but he batted her hands away.

"Not yet, little cat." His voice had become deeper, almost a growl.

She pouted, and he laughed.

"I have other plans for you." He took her hand and led her to the bathroom.

She followed him inside and gasped. Like her bathroom, the entire room was designed to get wet. But unlike hers, T'arq's bathroom had showerheads mounted to the walls and ceiling in one corner, a toilet was to one side, and a sink was mounted into the wall next to it. There was a rack holding fluffy towels and soap dispensers held liquids of different colors.

"This is way better than mine."

T'arq pressed a panel on the wall and water poured from the showerheads. Within seconds steam had filled the bathroom. He turned toward her and reached to unclasp her bra and slide it from her arms. She pushed the sides of her panties down and kicked them away.

He led her under the spray and turned her around so her back was to his front. He reached for one of the soap dispensers and lathered her hair. His fingers slowly worked into her scalp and her head fell back on his shoulder, eyes closed.

"That feels so good." She moaned as he worked, smiling lightly at the chuckle that she felt through his chest more than heard. She lost all sense of time as his deft hands slid over her body, over her shoulders and arms, down her back and over her hips, down her legs, which felt unsteady.

At the push of a button, a bench emerged from the wall and he lifted one of her legs to rest her foot on it. He held her to him, one big hand braced against her stomach, as the other completed its tortuous worship of her body, never quite touching her where she wanted him to.

"T'arq," she moaned, her hands sliding up to reach for his head and pull his mouth down to hers. "Please." She gasped.

"Please?"

She mewled impatiently. "Please... stop..."

His hands stilled.

"Don't stop, just..."

His hands started moving again, achingly slowly. There was a smile in his voice when he spoke, his mouth near her ear, sending goosebumps over her skin. "What is it, little one? What do you need?"

She spun in his grip, soapy wet skin on soapy wet skin. "I need you."

"I'm here." He spread his hands wide and smirked.

She pursed her lips. "You know what I mean."

"Do I?"

The steam now filled the bathroom, and she pouted as he laughed.

"Do you want me to kiss you?"

"Yes."

He dropped his head and nuzzled her neck below her ear before nipping her lightly with his teeth. She moaned, her head rolling on her shoulders. T'arq slid a hand into her hair to hold her still before dropping his mouth onto hers in a kiss so light she hardly felt it. She tried to move closer, but he held her still, watching with his eyes open as he caught her bottom lip between his teeth.

"Oh!" Her eyes fluttered as she gave in to him.

"That's it, little one. Let me make you feel good." His hands reached to cup the heavy weight of her breasts, the nipples hardening against his palms.

"Do you want me to lick your sweet... pussy until you scream?" He pinched one nipple between his fingers, making her stiffen and jerk in his hands, then he soothed it with a lick.

"Oh god, yes!" She felt boneless and weak, letting him arrange her how he wanted. He settled her down to sit, spreading her legs wide and planting her feet on the bench. She felt a moment of panic at being so exposed and tried to close her legs, but as soon as his hands settled on her inner thighs, she relaxed, letting her knees open.

"Look at you. Just dripping for me. You're a dream come

true, little cat." His voice dropped in pitch as he spoke, hands sliding slowly up her inner thighs until his thumbs reached right where she wanted him.

Her hips jerked, trying to pull closer, and he chuckled and held her still. "So eager for me?"

"I want... I need... T'arq!" She lost all sense of anything except his hands on her, his breath on her skin, and then he was right there.

At the first touch of his tongue, she jumped, and then moaned as he tasted every part of her. One hand spread her open to him, while the other found her sensitive rear entrance.

Her eyes flew open. "T'arq? What—"

"Let me show you how good you can feel."

She nodded. "All right."

"Relax and just feel." He said, then smiled, lowering his head between her legs once more. Soon she was writhing and moaning, his fingers in places she had never thought would feel good, his tongue doing wicked things.

"Oh, fuck!" she cried out as the first waves of pleasure hit her, sending her topping into a mindless state. Krystal was vaguely aware of mumbling incoherent things before T'arq turned, eased her feet back to the floor and, turning the water off, wrapped her in a fluffy towel.

He picked her up as if she weighed nothing and carried her into the main room to place her on his bed. She watched as he toweled himself dry, completely unselfconscious about being naked. She was mesmerized by the way he moved, efficient but as lithe as a dancer. Her eyes followed the lines of muscle as he lifted his hands to towel off his hair, sending his back rippling.

Turning, he caught her watching him and his eyes heated. "Like what you see, little cat?"

She nodded, then looked down and dragged the towel tighter around her.

"What's wrong?" He was immediately there, tipping her chin back to look into her eyes with concerned ones of his own.

"It's just that you're very..." she waved a hand at him, "... and I'm all..." she waved her hand at herself.

He sat next to her on the bed, his thick thigh dwarfing hers. "I don't understand." His brows drew together.

"I'm nothing like you!" she burst out.

He smiled grimly. "I know I'm not good enough for you, but I hoped—"

She stood, clasping the towel to her chest, wet hair hanging around her shoulders. "What? You are perfect! It's as if every single celebrity that I have ever lusted after was rolled into one package. That's you. Women like me don't belong with guys like you."

"Women like you?"

She either didn't notice his stern tone or ignored it. "I'm fat, T'arq. I am not conventionally attractive. I have an ass that jiggles when I walk, let alone when I run. My hair won't behave. I have brown eyes. Brown! And I'm short. And you... you could have anyone, male or female."

T'arq's eyes narrowed with every word she spoke. "Trust that when I say these words that they are true. You are beautiful. Your curves are made for my hands to hold, and when you move, I cannot breathe for the way you light me up inside. Your breasts," he growled the word, "are perfect." His hand moved to grasp the corner of the towel, looking to her for permission before tugging gently to expose them. His hands reached to cup their weight, thumbs finding her nipples and brushing over them, back and forth. "They fill my hands so beautifully, Krystal."

She felt a little of the anxiety she had felt disappear at his words, at his touch.

"And your hair? It's wild and free, just like you." He smiled. "Your eyes have a beautiful dark rim around them and, right in the center, they're green in some lights."

She gaped at him.

"And, your height?" He stood, towering over her. Her head barely reached the middle of his chest. "I quite like the differences between us." His hands slid down to circle her waist and lift her against him, her legs wrapping around his waist as she settled against him, his hard cock trapped between her wet core and his stomach. Her towel slipped to the ground with a damp thud, ignored.

His lips found hers in a kiss so tender her heart ached. He pulled away, his expression unguarded and raw, and a little nervous. "Yes, I have had male and female lovers. But I have never felt this way before. Not with anyone. But I need to know if you can come to care for me, too."

CHAPTER TWENTY-THREE

T'arq

His heart thudded in his chest as if he had just attacked an entire fleet of Xakul fighters on his own. He licked his lips and watched her face as she processed his words.

"Oh, T'arq," she said with a small smile, her hand lifting to cup the side of his face.

His heart clenched, and he hated that he couldn't resist leaning into her touch.

He was such a hypocrite. He knew he had a reputation for being emotionally unavailable, and then he gets a taste of his own medicine and can't handle it? Great. Just great.

He eased Krystal to her feet and turned away, feeling suddenly uncertain.

"T'arq?" Her voice was small.

"Mmm?" he replied, not trusting himself to speak lest he give himself away.

"Look at me, please?" She touched him lightly on the arm and he turned, unable to resist her.

She stared up at him with those brown eyes, so soulful and deep. He found himself lost and almost missed the next words she spoke.

"Sorry, what?" His heart jerked in his chest as hope bloomed in him.

Did she just... No. Surely not.

"I have been drawn to you from the first moment I saw you." She smiled, her mouth kicking up more on one side than the other.

He held his breath.

"I didn't realize it at first. I knew I was attracted to you, but it was more than that." She slid her hand down his arm to clasp his hand in hers. She looked down at their joined hands. "And each time I saw you, I fell a little deeper until I was drowning in everything that is you."

Relief flooded through T'arq.

She smiled up at him and he gripped her around the waist and spun her around. He put her down and then sat on the edge of the bed, tugging her between his open knees.

"I want to discover everything there is to know about you, Krystal." He brushed her hair back from her forehead. "There's no rush. We have plenty of time."

"What are we going to discover first?" She leaned in and placed her hands on his shoulders.

T'arq slid a hand into her hair and angled her head just the way he wanted. He stopped, his lips brushing against hers as he spoke. "How it feels as I slide myself inside you?"

Her tongue darted out to wet her lips as she nodded, eyes wide.

"And just how many different noises you make as you come all over my cock?"

She shivered and stepped closer into the cradle of his legs, trying to brush her chest against his. "Yes, please," she said timidly.

He eased her closer and lifted her so her knees were on either side of his hips, her wet core pressing against him. He slid a hand between them to find her sopping entrance, sliding a finger inside her and watching her face as her eyelids flickered and her mouth dropped open. She bit her lip and let her head fall backwards over the arm he slid up to hold her. He bent her back slightly, watching as his finger delved into her, his thumb finding her clit and smoothing over it in wet circles.

Krystal's fingers tightened on his shoulders, her nails biting into his skin and leaving little half-moon marks. He grinned. Little cat, indeed.

Soon she was thrusting her hips toward him, little whimpers coming from her as she found a rhythm and rode his hand.

"That's it. Take what you need from me." T'arq ground out as he slid another finger inside her, her tight walls clamping down on his digits. "Relax. Let me help you get there." He felt her ease, and he scissored his fingers slightly, easing her open for what was to come. "Good girl, that's it. Soon you'll be stuffed full of my cock."

She cried out at his words, and he smirked. Oh, she liked the way he talked, did she? Good to know.

He pressed against the front wall of her pussy with his fingers, and she moaned. "You like that, do you? I have so many things planned for you, little one. You're going to take my cock like you were made for me. I'm going to feed it to you until you're begging me to fuck you."

She whimpered and clutched him harder, falling forward to rest her head on his shoulder as her hips moved frantically. T'arq's cock jerked at the noises she was making, the tip leaking and running down the length down to his balls.

Gritting his teeth, he ignored his own need, refocusing on his lapful of woman nearing her release. A little closer and she would come all over his hands.

"What if I was to tie you up?" Her head lifted and her eyes met his, pupils blown as she tried to focus on him. "You'd like that, wouldn't you? Unable to move, just endure whatever I wanted to do to you."

"Oh, fuck!" she cried, the first spasms of her orgasm clenching his thrusting fingers tight. He slipped his fingers free, and she grumbled in protest.

"You're such a good girl, Krystal. Taking whatever I give you." He smoothed a hand down her back as he lifted his hand to his mouth and slowly licked his fingers clean.

She watched, transfixed, as his cheeks hollowed as he sucked each finger, one by one. Releasing the final one with a smirk, he gripped her hips. "I'm going to fuck you now."

"Finally." She lifted herself onto her knees and reached for his cock. Her small hands were torturous on him, and he bit back a moan as she fisted his length and lined him up with her opening. He held her up, not letting her sink down onto him until she was whimpering and moaning and, finally, begging. "Please, T'arq. I need you inside me!"

"Since you asked so nicely." He eased himself into her, letting her slide down his hardness with agonizing slowness, until they were pelvis to pelvis. Her pussy gripped him with delicious little waves as he slid out a little and then back in, testing how much movement she could take.

She rested her head on his chest, panting. "You're so big."

"Is it too much?"

"Oh, no." She lifted her head to his. "It's—you are—perfect." She lifted her hips and he let her take control, finding a rhythm she wanted and taking her pleasure on him.

He fought to keep his hips still, not wanting to thrust upwards unexpectedly and hurt her. He knew he was large and she was not, and it could take some getting used to. But so far? She was doing admirably.

It wasn't long before her breathing became irregular, and she bit her lip. Her hips lost their rhythm and, with a cry she came, the pulses of her release almost sending him over the edge. She flopped into his arms, tilting her head backwards to giggle.

"That was..."

"That good, huh?"

"Mmm-hmm." She snuggled her head into him, but squealed as he picked her up, still buried inside her, and turned to lie down on top of her on the bed.

"We're not done yet, little cat." He grabbed a couple of pillows, and lifting her, placed them under her ass. "Perfect," he said as he admired the sight in front of him. She was splayed out across the bed, her arms tossed over her head, her hair a messy halo. Her gorgeous body was spread before him, her hips lifted to meet his where they were joined.

He pushed her thighs further apart with his hands, holding her legs open as he gazed at where his cock disappeared into her body. As he withdrew he could see his dick glisten with her wetness and he groaned, sliding home again and falling forward over her, arms braced either side of her head.

"Are you ready, little one? I don't think I have it in me to be gentle right now. I need you." He brushed a kiss on her lips.

"T'arq, I won't break." She smiled at him and pulled his head down to hers, sliding her tongue into his mouth.

He tried to begin slowly, but soon his hips found a rhythm that had him gasping and Krystal writhing underneath him. He eased back to sit on his heels, bringing Krystal with him. Her hands came to his shoulders and his to her hips as he raised and lowered her, fucking himself into her.

"That's it. Use me like I used you. I'm yours," she said, her words panted with uneven breaths.

He groaned and did as she asked, thrusting his hips up into her as he pulled her down, her breasts crushed against his chest. She tightened around him, sending him over and into his release. He flopped sideways, taking Krystal with him, but using the last of his energy to make sure she landed on top of him.

They lay panting, a sprawl of arms and legs. As their breath came back to normal, he eased himself from her.

"Oh, there's a lot." Krystal looked down at the pool that had spilled onto her thighs.

"I can fix that." T'arq found himself strangely possessive in the aftermath and dragged his fingers through the sticky mess to slide it back inside her. He watched her face as she followed his hand with her eyes, her mouth open. He pushed as much as he could inside her and then surveyed his handiwork with a smirk. "Perfect."

She lay back with a dazed look on her face, legs splayed

and his seed smeared on the inside of her thighs. The sight was enough to have his dick twitching.

"Look at you." He traced a finger from her throat, between her breasts, circling one nipple and then the other, before tracing down to her navel. He paused over her dripping pussy. Admiring the sight of his seed spread over her, tangled in the cropped brown curls that covered her. He traced his fingers down the insides of her legs, spreading her open once more.

Her eyes opened as she watched him. "T'arq..." she moaned.

"Yes, little one?" His fingers toyed with her clit and she gasped, eyes rolling back before she forced herself to look at him again.

"Can we do that again?"

"You're not too sore?" He didn't want her to feel any pain. Well, not unless it was delivered on purpose and she wanted it.

"No." She eased away from him to slide onto her hands and knees, dropping her chest to the bed and wiggling her generous ass at him.

His cock, already hard, became like the hardest steel at the sight that was before him. "It's a good thing that I'm only part Taurean, little cat." He slid a hand over her ass to push her toward the mattress.

"Only part Taurean? Is that why your eyes are purple?" Krystal turned her head to look at him.

He lay next to her, pulling her into the crook of his arm. "That's part of it."

She snuggled into him, tracing lazy circles on his chest. "What's the rest?"

T'arq felt oddly at ease in a way he never had. Talking about his heritage was not something he did, not even with his mother, but with Krystal. "My mother is Taurean, but my father's parentage is mixed." He felt a sense of peace wash over him as he spoke. "My grandmother was from Felicina, and she met my grandfather when she was working on a deep space cargo freighter. They fell in love."

Krystal's eyebrows drew together. "Is Felicina that planet where people have tails?"

T'arq grinned. "Yes. And my parents were worried that I would have a tail, like my father did, but all I got were these eyes," he waved toward his face, "and the fur."

"You don't talk about this, do you?" she asked.

"No. It was hard as a child. My mother was disowned by her family for marrying my father, so they moved to the outer planets."

"That's awful. That must have been terrible."

"It wasn't until they sent me to the Taurean military academy. The outer planets are a melting pot of different races and cultures. If it wasn't such an unsafe place to live with the mercenary attacks and threat of the Xakul it would be perfect. But my parents wanted more opportunities than what I could get out there, so I worked hard and got a scholarship."

"Oh, T'arq." Krystal brushed a hand over his face. "You've come so far."

He shrugged.

She rolled onto her side to face him, resting a hand on his chest. "So, what's next?"

EPILOGUE
SIX WEEKS LATER

Krystal

So much had happened since Krystal had left Earth. When she stopped to think about it, she could hardly believe it.

In the weeks that had followed the destruction of the Xakul fake asteroid base, the team had been kept busy with follow up missions. The Zataras, along with several other Taurean starships, had formed a protective cordon around Earth, ready for the inevitable Xakul attack. There had been some stray Xakul fighters hiding in the asteroid field to capture, and more strange technology to destroy.

When she wasn't on a mission, she was working on further refinements to the cloak and training other engineers so the technology could be rolled out fleet wide. Krystal had overcome her fear of being in space, her fear of flying in a tiny spaceship, and had been on a dozen missions now, each one a little easier than the last. She wasn't entirely over her fear, but with T'arq beside her, she knew she would get there.

They'd been so busy that she'd barely had time to herself, let alone time alone with T'arq. A few snatched moments here and there left little opportunity for romance.

Until now.

The Zataras had docked for maintenance at the space station orbiting Taurus for the first time in months. All but the most essential crew had been given two day's leave, most heading directly to the planet's surface to see family.

Laila and Zac had gone to see Zac's parents, Oren and Domik had quickly transported to see their family, and CJ and Amelia had made a girls' weekend of it at a beach resort. Krystal had been tempted to join them, but wanted to spend the time alone with T'arq instead. That had been arranged with the help of Karik Za'Rell. Who would have thought the Supreme Commander himself was such a romantic? Not her, that's for sure.

It had been Karik who had held T'arq back in a meeting, allowing Krystal time to leave on a private shuttle, and Karik who had organized their destination—Irith's Moons.

Krystal peered out the window of the private shuttle, hands braced on the leather seat as she took her first look at the infamous resort.

Two large rings, stacked one on top of the other, formed the main section of the resort, like donuts, with several spokes leading toward a central, cylindrical tower. It was bright white, a shining beacon contrasting against the dark of space behind it. She had been told that the central tower was the public space, the two donuts able to be sectioned off for more private affairs. At the top and bottom of the tower a series of docks for shuttles were attached, and this is where Krystal's shuttle was headed.

Krystal smoothed a hand down the silky fabric of her dress, purple this time, and checked the time on her comm for what felt like the tenth time in as many minutes.

As far as T'arq knew, Krystal had gone to the beach resort with CJ and Amelia, and he was heading on yet another mission. Hopefully he would forgive her that one small lie when he saw what she had in store for him.

"Miss Krystal?"

She looked up to see the attendant holding out a tablet. She had been surprised to see a human woman on the flight, but quickly realized that, of course Karik Za'Rell's private shuttle would make use of humans. They had less connections on Taurus. Less people to tell about the comings and goings of the Supreme Commander. It was a logical security measure.

"A message for you."

"Thank you, Kate," she said, taking the device with a nod and checking the contents.

T'arq had left a scant few hours after her and was making better time than she was. They would likely arrive on Irith's Moons at the same time. She'd soon find out.

Docking was quick, Krystal quickly disembarking to be greeted by the Taurean equivalent of a concierge.

"Miss Krystal? Please, follow me," the Taurean man was not built like the warriors she was used to seeing on the Zataras. Instead, he was a little shorter, though still much taller than Krystal, and lean. His long limbs were encased in a dark gray uniform, similar to a tuxedo, with a bright white shirt underneath the jacket.

Krystal paused to read the name badge pinned to his chest. "Thank you, Ja'Kell."

He smiled and turned, gesturing for her to follow him. Her dress slid over her legs as she moved, the pumps she had replicated to match her dress sinking into the plush, cream-colored carpet with every step. For once, the air was a comfortable temperature, a subtle nod to the expense of heating such a place in deep space. Her luggage followed on an automated trolley, hovering over the ground at a safe distance behind her.

Ja'Kell turned down one corridor, then another, to pause at a bank of elevators. "Here is your access code," he said, swiping a device over her outstretched wrist and programming her comm. "This will allow you to enter and leave as you wish, though please ask should you need anything." He swiped his wrist over the panel on the wall and the elevator doors opened. "This is your private elevator—"

Krystal's eyebrows shot up. "Private?"

"—yes, only you and Sub-Commander Qu'Ress have access."

"Oh." She peered into the small space. It looked like every other elevator she had ever seen, even on Earth. Just with more gold and marble.

"Please, enjoy your stay."

Krystal stepped into the space, her hovering luggage following her and the doors shutting silently behind her. When they opened, she gasped.

The luggage beeped impatiently behind her and Krystal took a dazed step forward and into the large open-plan living space, noting absently that her luggage was placed near what had to be the largest bed she had ever seen in her life. The trolley slid into the still open elevator before the doors closed and Krystal was left alone.

She turned slowly, taking it all in. The high ceilings were not the dull gray she was used to. Instead, they were a dark navy flecked with spots of light. She gasped, realizing the entire ceiling was made of viewscreens showing a night sky. There was no carpet, instead scattered rugs in more shades of pink than she knew existed were spread all over the wooden floor. To one side, a low couch faced what looked suspiciously like a fireplace.

A fireplace? Here?

Krystal walked closer, curious, and discovered it was an ingenious holographic display unlike anything she had seen. She laughed in surprise, becoming so drawn into its workings that she barely registered the elevator door opening behind her. She spun at the sound of booted feet on the wooden—was it really wood?—floor.

"T'arq," she cried and ran toward him, tripping on the long length of her skirt and tumbling toward the floor before being swung into his powerful arms.

"Steady, kitten." He chuckled, setting her on her feet and smoothing a hand down the silken length of her dress. He was still in his combat armor, the dark gray standing in stark contrast to the muted furnishings in the room. "What's all this?" He gestured with a hand to the room, his gaze stilling as he took in the bed.

"Um." She cleared her throat. "It's a surprise. For you. For us." She fiddled with her skirt, lifting and dropping the fabric between her fingers.

This had to be the scariest thing she had ever done.

"A surprise," he repeated, head tilted to one side as he bent to pull his boots off.

"Yes. We hardly see each other and I wanted to..." she

trailed off as she watched his hands go to the clasps on his armor and pull it loose to clatter to the floor in a pile.

"You wanted to...?"

Drat him. What was she saying?

"I wanted..."

He slid his arms free of his chest covering and dropped it to the ground, his hands going to the closure on his pants and snapping them open.

"You wanted?" He grinned, obviously enjoying her discomfiture as he slid the fabric down his legs to stand naked in front of her.

She spun away from him, turning her back and began speaking again. "See? You take your clothes off and I can't even think, let alone say what I want to say." She went so far as to stamp her foot in frustration, the lightweight shoe making hardly any noise, much to her annoyance.

"Pretend I am clothed then." His voice came from further away now and she turned to see him climbing onto the bed that filled the center of the room. His bronze skin stood out against the crisp, white sheets and she pressed a hand to her chest.

"But you're not!" She wailed.

He took pity on her and pulled the sheet up to cover his groin. "There. Better?"

"How can you look more indecent now than when you were naked?" She scowled.

"Come here, little cat. Tell me what's bothering you." He sat up against the mass of pillows and propped himself on one arm, patting the bed next to him.

She sighed and settled on the bed next to him. "I wanted

to surprise you. For us to go on a little holiday, just the two of us." She swallowed past the lump in her throat. "For us to talk."

The truth was neither of them had said those three little words.

T'arq smiled gently. "According to the esteemed Supreme Commander, I am to spend these two days doing whatever you wish me to do."

"He said that?" Krystal gaped.

T'arq nodded. "So, what is on your mind, Krystal?"

She sat in silence for long moments, twisting the sheet in her hands before setting it down and taking a shaky breath. "I have never felt this way about anyone before."

He nodded. "I feel the same way."

She turned to stare at him, knowing this moment would be important for them both. "T'arq, I love you."

He winked. "I know."

Her mouth dropped open, and she blinked again.

"You know?"

He grinned. "Yes. And I love you. With everything that I am."

"Oh."

His smile dropped, and his hand reached to take hers. "I understand. I am not who you deserve, but I am too selfish to stand by and watch you become the mate of someone else."

What was he saying? Her head swum. First, he loved her and now he was... what, exactly?

"I don't want anyone else."

"You don't?" His voice filled with such boyish hope that her chest felt tight.

"I only want you, T'arq."

His eyes took on a feral gleam, flashing from lilac to dark purple as he pulled her face toward his to capture her chin in his hand and touch his lips to hers. One, two feather light kisses. He deepened with a groan to slide his tongue between her lips and taste her. She felt light-headed and slid her hands behind his head to clutch at the back of his neck.

She pulled away, breaths coming quickly. "I have one rule."

He raised an eyebrow.

"Promise me you won't decide what's best for me without speaking to me."

He nodded solemnly. "I promise."

She grinned, throwing her arms around his neck. Her mouth met his, and he rolled her underneath him, settling his big body on top of hers. And for a long while afterwards, conversation was not on either of their minds.

The End

———

Thank you for reading Alien Seduction!

Please consider giving a rating or leaving a review, it's what helps readers find books they love, and I appreciate every single one.

———

The next book in the Taurean Warriors Series is Alien Domination, and is Domik and CJ's story.

Read on to find out more!

ALIEN DOMINATION
GRUMPY ALIEN MEETS SUNSHINE HUMAN.
CHAOS ENSUES.

If there's one thing life has taught battlefield medic CJ, it's to not get involved. And to absolutely never fall in love. Ever.

Especially not with a big, strong, stoic alien hottie. One she can't resist teasing to make smile.

So why, when everything goes to shit and he wraps her in his arms, does she feel like getting involved might be exactly what she needs?

Find out more
www.melodybeckett.com/taurean-warriors

———

Do you want to know exactly how Oren and Amelia first met?

Read on to find out...

ALIEN ATTRACTION

SHE DOESN'T BELIEVE ALIENS EXIST... UNTIL ONE NEEDS HER HELP.

Commander Oren Ka'Ress is having a bad day. First he crash lands on a primitive planet and is injured in the crash, then he—and his dangerous Xakul prisoner—are captured. Oren needs backup, but with no way to contact his fellow Taureans, he's stuck.

Dr. Amelia O'Malley doesn't believe in aliens... until a mysterious patient arrives on her ward. Bigger than any man she's ever seen, and with inhumanly bright eyes, Amelia finds herself full of questions. But there's one problem—Amelia can't understand anything he says.

As the Xakul threat looms, Oren must find a way for Amelia to understand him. With the clock counting down there is more at stake than either of them could dream...

———

Download your FREE eBook when you join Melody's
newsletter.

www.melodybeckett.com/newsletter

ACKNOWLEDGMENTS

This book was such fun to write. I really adore T'arq and his filthy, filthy mouth! Some of the things he wanted to say surprised me, but who am I to deny a character their agency? It did make for a couple of interesting conversations with Mr B, who does my proof reading! Thank you, my love. Your unending support and encouragement means more than I can say.

My editor, Tiffany of Write Now Creative, did such a fantastic job on this manuscript. Thank you, your constructive feedback is always spot on.

A very big thanks is owed to Ursa Dax, who helped me work through some issues with the title of this book. She's a talented writer and, if you haven't already, you should go check out her books.

And, as always, thank you to you. My reader. I am so very thankful that you took a chance on this book. :)

Happy reading!

Mel xx

ABOUT THE AUTHOR

Melody has been a voracious reader of anything with a happy ending since she was old enough to pick up a book. As a teenager she pulled all-nighters reading romance novels under the covers with a torch. She still reads like a fiend, and can always be found with her e-reader within reach!

As a writer, she pens the stories her teenage self wished existed: stories that marry her love for science fiction, action movies, and romance, and stories with happy ever afters.

She hopes you enjoy reading them as much as she enjoys writing them for you!

To keep up to date with Melody's writing and for special offers, sign up to her newsletter.

www.melodybeckett.com/newsletter

ALSO BY MELODY BECKETT

Taurean Warriors Series

Alien Attraction

Alien Desire

Alien Seduction

Alien Domination

Other works

An Alien For Christmas